Upside Down

By Danielle Steel

UPSIDE DOWN · THE BALL AT VERSAILLES · SECOND ACT · HAPPINESS · PALAZZO
THE WEDDING PLANNER · WORTHY OPPONENTS · WITHOUT A TRACE
THE WHITTIERS · THE HIGH NOTES · THE CHALLENGE · SUSPECTS · BEAUTIFUL
HIGH STAKES · INVISIBLE · FLYING ANGELS · THE BUTLER · COMPLICATIONS
NINE LIVES · FINDING ASHLEY · THE AFFAIR · NEIGHBORS · ALL THAT GLITTERS
ROYAL · DADDY'S GIRLS · THE WEDDING DRESS · THE NUMBERS GAME
MORAL COMPASS · SPY · CHILD'S PLAY · THE DARK SIDE · LOST AND FOUND
BLESSING IN DISGUISE · SILENT NIGHT · TURNING POINT · BEAUCHAMP HALL
IN HIS FATHER'S FOOTSTEPS · THE GOOD FIGHT · THE CAST · ACCIDENTAL HEROES
FALL FROM GRACE · PAST PERFECT · FAIRYTALE · THE RIGHT TIME · THE DUCHESS
AGAINST ALL ODDS · DANGEROUS GAMES · THE MISTRESS · THE AWARD
RUSHING WATERS · MAGIC · THE APARTMENT · PROPERTY OF A NOBLEWOMAN
BLUE · PRECIOUS GIFTS · UNDERCOVER · COUNTRY · PRODIGAL SON · PEGASUS
A PERFECT LIFE · POWER PLAY · WINNERS · FIRST SIGHT · UNTIL THE END OF TIME
THE SINS OF THE MOTHER · FRIENDS FOREVER · BETRAYAL · HOTEL VENDÔME
HAPPY BIRTHDAY · 44 CHARLES STREET · LEGACY · FAMILY TIES · BIG GIRL
SOUTHERN LIGHTS · MATTERS OF THE HEART · ONE DAY AT A TIME
A GOOD WOMAN · ROGUE · HONOR THYSELF · AMAZING GRACE · BUNGALOW 2
SISTERS · H.R.H. · COMING OUT · THE HOUSE · TOXIC BACHELORS · MIRACLE
IMPOSSIBLE · ECHOES · SECOND CHANCE · RANSOM · SAFE HARBOUR
JOHNNY ANGEL · DATING GAME · ANSWERED PRAYERS · SUNSET IN ST. TROPEZ
THE COTTAGE · THE KISS · LEAP OF FAITH · LONE EAGLE · JOURNEY
THE HOUSE ON HOPE STREET · THE WEDDING · IRRESISTIBLE FORCES
GRANNY DAN · BITTERSWEET · MIRROR IMAGE · THE KLONE AND I
THE LONG ROAD HOME · THE GHOST · SPECIAL DELIVERY · THE RANCH
SILENT HONOR · MALICE · FIVE DAYS IN PARIS · LIGHTNING · WINGS · THE GIFT
ACCIDENT · VANISHED · MIXED BLESSINGS · JEWELS · NO GREATER LOVE
HEARTBEAT · MESSAGE FROM NAM · DADDY · STAR · ZOYA · KALEIDOSCOPE
FINE THINGS · WANDERLUST · SECRETS · FAMILY ALBUM · FULL CIRCLE
CHANGES · THURSTON HOUSE · CROSSINGS · ONCE IN A LIFETIME
A PERFECT STRANGER · REMEMBRANCE · PALOMINO · LOVE: *POEMS* · THE RING
LOVING · TO LOVE AGAIN · SUMMER'S END · SEASON OF PASSION · THE PROMISE
NOW AND FOREVER · PASSION'S PROMISE · GOING HOME

Nonfiction

EXPECT A MIRACLE: *Quotations to Live and Love By*
PURE JOY: *The Dogs We Love*
A GIFT OF HOPE: *Helping the Homeless*
HIS BRIGHT LIGHT: *The Story of Nick Traina*

For Children

PRETTY MINNIE IN PARIS
PRETTY MINNIE IN HOLLYWOOD

DANIELLE STEEL

Upside Down

A Novel

Delacorte Press

New York

Published in the United States by Delacorte Press, an imprint of Random House, a division of Penguin Random House LLC, New York.

DELACORTE PRESS is a registered trademark and the DP colophon is a trademark of Penguin Random House LLC.

Hardback ISBN 978-0-593-49837-8
Ebook ISBN 978-0-593-49838-5

Printed in the United States of America on acid-free paper

randomhousebooks.com

2 4 6 8 9 7 5 3 1

First Edition

To my beloved children,
Trevor, Todd, Beatrix, Nick, Samantha,
Victoria, Vanessa, Maxx, and Zara,

May you each find your soul mate,
and be brave enough to love them, when you do.

May life bless you in every possible way,
and bring you safety, peace, and joy.

I love you with all my heart, always.

Mom/d.s.

Upside Down

Chapter 1

The line of limousines snaked down the driveway of the Beverly Hilton hotel at a snail's pace to drop off stars and starlets, producers, directors, ingénues, the famous and the infamous and the unknowns and wannabes, desperate to be seen at one of Hollywood's most glittering annual events, the Golden Globe Awards. The greatly respected award was second only to the Academy Awards. At sixty-two, Ardith Law, one of Hollywood's biggest stars for the past forty years, had won three Golden Globes so far. And she had two of the Academy's coveted Oscars to her credit as well. This was an evening she never missed, as much to pay her respects to her fellow actors as to be seen herself. It was one of those things one had to do. It was expected, and you had to keep your face out there if you wanted to continue to get work, and your face had to look damn good or you'd better not show up!

Ardith was known for the variety and depth of the roles she accepted, and the quality of the movies she starred in. Occasionally, she took a small, unusual part if it intrigued her, which happened from time to time, but as a rule, she only took major starring roles. She was an extraordinary actress with a huge talent and a well-deserved reputation. She was picky about the parts she took. She wanted to be in movies with depth and merit, which weren't always easy to find after a certain age. She looked exceptionally good at sixty-two, was still beautiful, and unlike nearly every actress in Hollywood, she had had no "work" done. She preferred to keep her own natural face and left it to the makeup artists on set to correct whatever needed attention. And she was never afraid to take an important part if it aged her beyond her actual years.

Ardith wanted roles with substance that stretched her to the limits of her abilities. She turned down most of the easy parts. Although for the past two years, there had been no offers. No one dared to cast her in minor roles, and producers knew that her agent, Joe Ricci, would turn them down before the offers even got to her. But once she turned sixty, there had been no appropriate parts for her. She read scripts constantly, looking for the right roles, but hadn't seen any she wanted to play. Her high standards and perfectionism on set had won her the reputation of being difficult or a diva, which wasn't entirely true. She was an extremely dedicated actress and demanded a lot of herself and everyone she worked with. So now and then, when others fell short, forty years of the best parts available and producers who would do almost anything to keep her happy had led to rare but memorable outbursts that supported the notion that she was a diva. She was above all a consummate professional, and a star to her very core. It wasn't about ego, but more about wanting to be the absolute best she could be in every role, at all times. She hated working with lazy actors, and she hated stupidity and phonies. She was true to herself and her high standards in every way. She was an honest woman, and a great actress more than a diva, no matter what people said who didn't really know her. Her career was vital to her sense of well-being and purpose. She had missed working for the past two years but preferred it to accepting roles in second-rate movies. She was waiting for the right film to come along, and she knew that eventually it would. In the meantime, she read every book and script she could lay her hands on.

Her personal life had always taken a back seat to her career, and it still did. She had one daughter from an eight-year marriage that began in her twenties. She had been married to one of Hollywood's biggest producers, John Walker. They had been a powerful pair and had made several movies together, which had been legendary box office successes and enhanced both their careers. It had been a tumultuous but creative match, which also produced their only daughter, Morgan, who was now thirty-eight years old and a plastic surgeon in New York.

Morgan had avoided the Hollywood scene all her life, and chose medicine as an exciting, satisfying alternative. It suited her. She was a partner in a successful practice of plastic surgeons, with two senior partners who had worked together for years. One was close to retirement, the other was in full swing, and Morgan was the only woman they had ever invited to join the partnership. One of the senior partners also taught at Columbia medical school. They set the bar high.

Ardith wished now that she had spent more time with Morgan when she was younger, but her own career had been white-hot then, and she was too often away on location and away from Morgan, and didn't deny it. Ardith had missed all the important moments and landmarks in Morgan's life, the school plays, her first prom, her first heartbreak, many birthdays, and there was no way to catch up. She felt guilty about it now but there was no way to make up for it, or relive the past. Once Morgan was an adult, the two women were very different. Morgan respected her mother's career but had never enjoyed it, and the differences in their personalities and respective careers were hard to bridge now. They spoke often, out of duty and respect, but agreed on very little. Morgan had few memories of her father, who had died when she was seven. There had been scandal around her father's death, which had troubled her for years.

John Walker had died in a tragic helicopter accident, which was even more traumatic for Ardith because he was killed with the young woman he was rumored to be having an affair with at the time, a budding actress who was appearing in one of his movies and whose career he was shepherding. She was twenty-two, and Ardith was thirty-one then. The letters she found after John's death with his protégée confirmed her fears and suspicions about their involvement. Ardith had never forgiven him for it. The press had turned his death into a lurid event. Morgan knew the story once she was older, and had harbored illusions about him anyway. His films remained as tributes to him, but his reputation as a womanizer lasted after his death. Ardith knew it wasn't his first affair by any means and had said as much to Morgan. He could never resist the actresses in his films. Ardith had never married again and had no regrets that she hadn't. It was an experience she never wanted to repeat, as she had no desire to be married to another cheater and she didn't want more children. Morgan was enough to deal with on her own, and their relationship had never been easy, and less and less so when Morgan grew up. She'd been rebellious in her teens, and angry about the parents she didn't have. Ardith readily admitted that although she loved her daughter, motherhood wasn't her strong suit. Morgan agreed. Ardith hadn't been prepared for how much she needed to give a child, especially after her father died. They occasionally had a good time together, but they didn't see each other often anymore. Ardith had the time to give her now, but Morgan didn't have the interest or the time. She was busy with her career as a physician in New York, and her mother was proud of her, but Ardith still had her own life as a star in L.A. Morgan was single at thirty-eight and said she didn't have time for a husband and children, or even dating. Her work and her patients were her priorities. In some ways she was like her mother—her career came first. And the tables had turned. Ardith hadn't made enough time for her when she was a child, and now Morgan made no effort for her. It was a cycle they couldn't seem to break, and Ardith had accepted the fact that it was too late and they would never be close. They existed on the periphery of each other's lives. And living on opposite coasts, they saw too little of each other to heal the damage of the past. They had the occasional nice dinner together, and then Morgan flew back to New York, and they didn't see each other for months.

For the past twelve years, Ardith had found comfortable companionship with William West, who was almost as big a star as she was. He had been a readily identifiable hero over a fifty-year career, even longer than Ardith's. He had never won an Oscar, and hadn't taken the challenging roles she had, but audiences loved him. He took parts that endeared him to his fans. Since he wasn't as demanding about the parts he played, he worked more often than Ardith, and still did one or two pictures a year. He was leaving in two days for England on location, playing a worthwhile role, although he was no longer the romantic lead. At seventy-eight, he was healthy and energetic and wanted to continue working, even in slightly less important parts. He had no desire to retire.

Ardith always said that the sixteen-year age difference between them didn't bother her. When they'd gotten together, she was fifty and he was sixty-six, still a handsome man, and a star. They had their careers in common, and he was kind, attentive, and good company. He had slowed down a little in the past few years, but other than the handful of pills and vitamins she handed him every day to keep him healthy, he was in surprisingly good condition for his age. No one knew what would come later, but for now he was doing fine and still working. He hadn't been as wise with money as she was. He had never commanded the salaries she did and was grateful to be living in her home in Bel Air for the past ten years. He contributed a small amount to expenses, but Ardith didn't expect anything from him. He had been married and divorced twice, to actresses both times, had only stayed married briefly, and had no children, which kept things simple. He had always been friendly to Morgan, but she was already doing her residency at Columbia by the time he and Ardith got together, so Morgan's relationship with him was cordial but superficial. She had no complaints against him, he was friendly and polite and good to her mother, and he had appeared much too late to be a father figure to her. She said she had no need for one, and she found him somewhat narcissistic, like most actors, more concerned with his own looks, projects, and problems than anyone else's. Ardith was used to it and didn't mind, and they were each the longest relationship either of them had ever had. After twelve years, they had become a legendary Hollywood couple, and were always seen together. It wasn't a great love affair and never had been, but it was companionship for both of them. They had each other and weren't alone or lonely.

When the car finally stopped in front of the Hilton, Ardith stepped out of the car, in a long sleek black satin gown, which molded her impeccably maintained figure. She had a white fox wrap on her shoulders, was wearing a diamond necklace and earrings she had borrowed from Van Cleef & Arpels, and her blond hair was combed in a smooth, elegant bun. She looked dazzling, and the press went wild when they saw her, flashing her picture, shouting her name, waving to catch her attention as Bill West stepped out behind her in an impeccable tuxedo. She smiled and waved like royalty at the mass of photographers and the fans hovering near them at the edge of the crowd, and she and Bill glided smoothly inside to make their way down the red carpet before the dinner and award ceremony began. Once Ardith and Bill were in a room or a crowd, all eyes were on them. Most people assumed that they were married by now, but they weren't, and she still had no desire to be. She said there was no reason for it, although Bill reminded her from time to time that he would prefer it, but he was of a previous generation. And she always pointed out that at this point marriage wouldn't change anything. They had lived together for ten out of twelve years, and there was no additional benefit to marriage, except emotional reassurance she didn't need. Ardith was a strong, self-sufficient woman and preferred her life that way.

Bill had beaten prostate cancer five years before, which had left him healthy and cancer-free but unable to perform sexually, which she accepted. She was young to give up sex, but it was a sacrifice she made for him. The relationship they had suited her, and him as well. She couldn't imagine meeting someone else now and having to adjust to a new man. She had had enough men in her life and was satisfied to have Bill West be the last one. They were both Hollywood icons and thought to be the perfect couple. In some ways, being with a man his age aged her, and in others it made her feel young. They seemed right together in everyone's eyes, including their own. He was the perfect supporting actor to her, the star.

They spent half an hour going down the red carpet, then made their way to their table, where they would have dinner and watch the awards. The Golden Globes were important and often predicted how the Oscars would go two months later. Ardith and Bill were seated at a table of comparable major stars, and the TV cameras sought them out constantly. They would be under close scrutiny all night, and Bill had already told Ardith he wanted to go home right after the awards and skip the after-parties. He still had a lot to do before he left for England two days later, and he didn't want to stay out late, although she would have enjoyed it. She didn't want to go to the parties without him, so she planned to leave with him.

Ardith and Bill both accurately predicted who would win that night, and approved of the foreign press's choices, and after making their way back through the photographers, they escaped without attending any of the parties and were back at Ardith's house in Bel Air before midnight. Ardith had already packed most of what Bill would need in England, but he kept adding to it, afraid she had forgotten something. She was going to pack his various medications in his briefcase, with notes about what to take when. He fell asleep with his arm around her that night, with Oscar, Ardith's tiny white toy poodle, on the bed next to her. She took him everywhere, which Bill had objected to at first, but he finally got used to him. Ardith claimed the dog was her soulmate, and his constant presence was nonnegotiable.

Ardith was an early riser and was already at the breakfast table the next day when Bill appeared in a navy cashmere dressing gown with navy satin lapels. She looked up and smiled when she saw him. She read the *Los Angeles Times, The New York Times,* and *The Wall Street Journal* every day. She had an insatiable hunger for knowing about the world around her, more so than Bill, who read *Variety* for news of the film industry, which was all that really interested him. He said that he left Ardith in charge of world news, and was sure she'd let him know if the stock market crashed or a war broke out, and she promised she would.

"Did you sleep well?" she asked him, as she did every morning, with a tender look.

"I did." He smiled at her. "I hate to leave you for two months," he said wistfully, as she poured him a cup of coffee. But he had no desire to retire either. He enjoyed his work and loved going on location. It made him feel busy and alive, and important. "I had an email from the producer this morning. Your assistant starts tomorrow, when I leave." As part of his contract, and to induce him to go on location for two months, the producers would provide an assistant to help Ardith with all the small tasks Bill did for her. He worried about her being alone for so long with no one to help her and felt mildly guilty leaving. He was still a bankable name and to keep him happy, the producers agreed to provide Ardith the assistant, she had guessed probably a young actress they knew well who wasn't currently working and needed the money. And she was grateful for whatever help an assistant would give her. She was expecting a female assistant. She had a housekeeper who came daily during the week, and left dinner for them if they weren't going out. Ardith often drove herself around town, but used drivers too. She drove Bill when he had appointments, or he took an Uber. She thought an assistant might be superfluous, but Bill wanted her to accept it. It was free and an add-on to his contract, which his agent had negotiated. It was a perk for her to share, so she agreed somewhat hesitantly. Since it wasn't Ardith's contract, they didn't offer her the opportunity to interview whoever they hired. She was mildly worried that an unknown assistant might be more of an annoyance than a help, but she could always fire her if she didn't like her, and it made Bill feel as though he had done something special for her, so she hadn't argued about it.

"Did they tell you anything about her?" Ardith asked, as she poured skim milk into a bowl of cereal for him. She watched his diet more carefully than he did. He would have preferred bacon and fried eggs, which she didn't allow him. There was a responsibility that went with being with a man his age. She was as much a nurse as a girlfriend.

"No, they didn't," he said about the assistant. "I'm sure she'll be very nice. You can send Oscar to the groomer with her," he said, a task which he personally didn't like. Oscar had never been overly fond of Bill. Oscar knew who his friends were. Bill wasn't a "dog person" and Oscar knew it.

"I don't mind taking him," Ardith said breezily.

"What are you hearing from Morgan these days?" he asked her. He was impressed by Morgan's medical career. Even though they weren't close, Ardith frequently asked her for medical advice, which Morgan was loath to give her. Ardith checked on all of Bill's medications with her daughter, to be sure there weren't dangerous side effects the doctors hadn't informed him of.

"Nothing much. All Morgan does is work," she answered his question.

"No man in her life?" He was sorry she hadn't met someone by now, at thirty-eight. He thought she should make some effort in that direction, as she wasn't getting any younger if she wanted a husband and a child. Bill had old-school views on every subject, particularly women and relationships.

"She says she doesn't have time," Ardith said. She had stopped reminding her daughter of it herself. It was up to Morgan if she wanted marriage and kids. It didn't look like it so far, and she loved her work. Morgan had never been very interested in marriage. "She's thinking about going to Vietnam this fall, to work on a special project, pro bono, helping kids with burns. It sounds awful, but noble."

"She's a good girl," Bill said admiringly, and left the table a short time later to finish packing. Ardith drove him all over town to do last-minute errands, and they were both exhausted that night when they went to bed. He had to leave the house at six A.M., as the producers were having him picked up for a nine A.M. flight to London. He was getting VIP treatment all the way, due to his age and status.

The alarm went off at five, and he was ready to leave when the car arrived. He looked lovingly at Ardith as they stood in the doorway, she in her nightgown, and Bill elegantly dressed for the trip.

He looked every inch a movie star, in a dark gray suit, blue shirt, and navy tie, with a well-cut navy overcoat, and a hat that made him look very dashing. He was excited to be going to work on a film for two months, and to have a good role, but he was sorry to leave her. She had promised to visit him in three weeks, and she was looking forward to some time alone while he was gone. She was planning to spend a night in New York on the way, to visit Morgan if her daughter had time. The plan wasn't definite yet. Morgan didn't make plans far in advance and said she was swamped at work.

"Try to behave while you're gone," Ardith teased Bill. "Don't fall in love with the star."

"You too," he said, and kissed her. He had more to worry about than she did, but they were faithful to each other. She stood waving from the doorway as the car pulled away, and she envied him for a minute. She would have liked to be leaving to work on a film on location, and hoped she would be one of these days, for the right movie. It made Bill feel useful and engaged to be working. He had three suitcases for his elegant suits, and a fourth one just for shoes. He had friends in London he planned to see when they had breaks, and he wouldn't be on set every day. The role wasn't too physically demanding, unlike the projects Ardith usually signed on for, which required months of preparation. His career had never been as demanding as hers. He was the only actor she'd ever been involved with who wasn't jealous of her and didn't punish her for her success, which was one of the reasons their relationship worked so well. He had never been resentful of her fame. Bill was easygoing, comfortable with who he was, satisfied with the degree of success he'd achieved, and didn't want more than that. Unlike Ardith, who had always pushed herself hard, physically and mentally, with the roles she took, always wanting to achieve more. It was why she had won two Oscars and he hadn't, and he didn't mind that either. At seventy-eight, he was just happy to still be in the game and to have work at all. He had never been as ambitious or driven as she was. They were a good fit that way.

She went back to bed, thinking about him after he left, happy for him that he would be working. It was an impressive cast, which would be fun, and a famous director whom Bill had worked with before.

She fell asleep, woke up two hours later, showered, and put on a green face mask she didn't like applying when Bill was at home. It made her look like the witch in *The Wizard of Oz*. Then she sat down to breakfast with the papers she read every day. She was halfway through the *Los Angeles Times* when there was the sound of an explosion outside, or some kind of major disturbance. She looked up in surprise, peeked through the blinds of the kitchen window, and saw an enormous motorcycle head straight for the house and spin around with a spray of gravel. The biker riding it looked like Darth Vader or a Hell's Angel, in a helmet with a black shield that concealed his face, a black motorcycle jacket, torn jeans, and biker boots, and he sat staring at the house for a minute, looking as though he was going to kill someone if he got inside. Benicia, the housekeeper, came running up to Ardith, looking terrified.

"He looks like a Hell's Angel, should I call the police?" she whispered, while Ardith tried to evaluate the situation and just how dangerous the biker was. He looked like a rough customer. Oscar was barking frantically from the noise the biker had already made with the Harley.

"Where are the panic buttons?" Ardith asked, whispering too. He looked menacing as he slowly got off the enormous motorcycle. You heard about guys like him, who broke into homes or held people at gunpoint while they robbed them in broad daylight.

Benicia took a panic button out of a drawer and handed it to Ardith, as she continued to watch him, wondering if he was armed or going to break a window to enter the house. It had never happened before. She didn't like guns and didn't keep one in the house, although Bill thought she should, for an event such as this. Burglars and criminals in the Los Angeles area were known to be pretty bold. Ardith was holding the panic button in her hand, about to press it, while watching what the fearsome-looking biker was going to do. He took the helmet off, and she saw that he was unshaven, with a face covered in beard stubble, and had longish hair that looked as though it hadn't seen a comb in months. He had a powerful build, and she had visions of him tying them up while he robbed the house. He didn't look like a drug addict, more like a thug. He was in good shape, with broad shoulders. He walked away from the kitchen windows, strode up the front steps, and rang the doorbell, which wasn't what she expected at all. Or maybe robbers were just that brazen now, they rang the front doorbell, grabbed you, and tied you up. She hit the panic button as soon as he rang the bell and tiptoed to the front door to get a better look at him through the peephole. He was just standing there, and she knew the police would arrive in less than ten minutes. Ardith told Benicia to stay in the kitchen—she didn't want her housekeeper getting hurt—and stood on the opposite side of the front door, wondering what to do before the police arrived. Bill had been gone for exactly three hours and they were under attack. She remembered then that he had told *Variety* that he was leaving town for two months on location, which she didn't like. Not that he would be any match for the hoodlum on their front steps, who was built like a bodybuilder and looked about thirty years old, if that, probably younger.

"Who is it?" Ardith shouted through the door, curious what he'd say, and trying to sound fierce herself. Her throat was dry, and she was shaking, but the adrenaline rush of fear made her brave.

"It's Josh Gray. Ms. Law's assistant," he said, sounding much meeker than Ardith as she let out a gasp and felt her knees go weak.

"You're *what*?" She unlocked and pulled open the door and stared at him, in her bathrobe and bare feet, with her hair piled on top of her head, and her face green with the forgotten face mask. She and the fierce-looking alleged assistant stared at each other in disbelief.

"I'm her new assistant . . . your new assistant," he said, hesitantly, assuming she was Ardith Law. "I'm supposed to start this morning. Mr. West's producer sent me."

"And you came to work looking like *that*?" she said with blatant disapproval. "I thought you were going to break into the house and kill us. And you're supposed to be a woman."

"Sorry, they sent me. For two months." Oscar the toy poodle ran into the hall from the kitchen and barked frantically at the man. Ardith could hear sirens in the distance, and in less than a minute, two squad cars arrived and four officers ran toward them with guns drawn, as Josh Gray looked panicked.

"Hands in the air," the police shouted at him, as one of them pushed him to the ground and he lay facedown on the lawn. Ardith looked embarrassed.

"I'm sorry," she said to the officers, as two of them stared at her. "It was a misunderstanding. I thought it was a break-in, but it was just my assistant coming to work." She tried to look starlike and sound charming and casual, as Josh looked up at them from the ground in shock, and she caught a glimpse of herself in the hall mirror and saw the green face mask she had forgotten. "Oh my God. I'm really sorry." The police withdrew quickly, and Josh got to his feet and stared at her. She was unrecognizable with the green goo on her face, but she was obviously Ardith Law. It was a hell of an introduction to his new boss, and he hadn't wanted the job anyway. Josh was an actor, out of work, his next movie had just been canceled so Bill's producer on the film assigned him to Ardith as an assistant for two months, which Josh had been dreading.

He had read about her reputation as a diva and had no desire to be her cabana boy for two months, but he was being paid to do it and he needed the money, since the sci-fi movie he'd been hired to do hadn't happened. But this was a lot worse than a bad movie. He was forty-one years old and had been acting in second-rate movies for the last ten years, and waiting on tables. He was still hoping for his big break, and it hadn't happened yet. Ardith Law was clearly not it.

"Come in," she said to him sternly, "before the whole neighborhood sees us." She picked up Oscar, Josh walked into the front hall, and she shut the door hard behind him. "What are you doing coming to work on that *thing*? You'll terrify the whole neighborhood. I thought you were a Hell's Angel."

"So you called the police?" He was still stunned at what had happened.

"You look dangerous. And why didn't they send a woman?"

"I think they were going to, but she got a part on some teen vampire movie, so you got me instead. The sci-fi movie I was supposed to do got canceled so I was free. I have a friend in the producer's office. He set me up for the job."

"Great. You look like Darth Vader. You can't come to work on that thing," she told him as he followed her into the kitchen, and Benicia stared at them both, unable to understand why Ardith had invited their attacker into the house.

"I don't have a car," he said politely, wondering if she was crazy, or just weird with the green face.

"Take an Uber. My neighbors will kill me for that racket. I can give you a car to drive while you're at work."

"What exactly am I going to be doing?" he asked, looking worried. "They said you needed an assistant while Mr. West is away."

"Exactly. You can take the dog to the groomer, pick up packages, do errands for me. Whatever I need," but having a male assistant was going to be a problem. He couldn't come into the room when she was undressed or take orders while she was in the bathtub. He wasn't what she wanted at all, and they had never told Bill they might send a man. He was almost useless to her.

"I'm not a trained bodyguard," he warned her.

"I don't need one. Or I didn't until you showed up. You scared poor Benicia to death," she scolded him. "And you have to come to work decently dressed, you can't run around town looking like a Hell's Angel. Do you have a jacket, like a blazer or something?"

He nodded. "Do you want me to wear a suit and tie?" he asked dismally.

"No, a proper shirt, clean untorn jeans, and a jacket will be fine, and real shoes or running shoes, no axe murderer boots." She looked at him with disapproval. "Do you like dogs?"

"I've never had one." Oscar was still barking, and Josh didn't look enthused at the prospect. "Does he bite?"

"Only people he doesn't like," Ardith said curtly. "He weighs three pounds. You don't need to worry about him." As she said it, Oscar bared his fangs and looked more like a rabid guinea pig than a dog. Josh looked miserable.

"Do you want me to go home and change?" She considered it, still in her green face, which she had forgotten again while berating him. He had upset them all, even the dog.

"You're fine for today. Try not to scare us to death tomorrow." He nodded, still remembering when he had been lying facedown on the lawn minutes before, with two armed LAPD officers pointing their guns at him. "I'll get dressed. You can run me into Beverly Hills to do some errands, that way I won't have to park."

"Fine." He nodded, still stunned by the first moments of his new job. The next eight weeks seemed frightening, given what he'd seen so far. A crazed mouse of a dog, a boss with a green face, armed police forcing him down on her front lawn. If he could have hit his own panic button, he would have. This was a lot worse than he had feared. She wasn't a diva, she was insane, and he was stuck with her for the next eight weeks. A drink to calm his nerves would have been appealing, and then maybe she'd fire him and he wouldn't have to deal with her for the next two months. But for now, he was on the hook, because his damn movie had been canceled and he had to be an errand boy to a lunatic. He wanted to run screaming out the door, but he knew he couldn't. He needed the money to pay his rent. Benicia looked at him suspiciously as he sat down at the kitchen table and waited for Ardith to reappear so he could drive her somewhere. As far as Josh was concerned, she needed an exorcist, not an assistant, and as he waited, he reached down to pet the frenzied toy poodle, who bared his fangs at him again, aspiring to be Cujo.

"Be nice," Josh whispered to him. "I'm not liking this any more than you are. I promise not to bother you if you don't bite me. Deal?" Oscar hesitated for a minute, stared Josh in the eye, uncurled his lips, and marched off to find his mistress, while Josh wondered what the production company would do to him if he quit on the first day. It was very tempting, and he wondered if he'd need a tetanus shot if Oscar bit him. This was definitely a high stress job, and not at all what he'd expected. But how much worse could it get? At least the cops didn't shoot him, but he couldn't bring his Harley to work, and he had to dress to cater to her. It was possibly the worst job he'd ever had, and diva didn't begin to describe it. A diva with a green face and a savage toy poodle. He couldn't wait to get home, smoke a joint, and have a martini. It was going to be a very, very long eight weeks working for Ms. Ardith Law!

Chapter 2

When Ardith came back to the kitchen half an hour later, she was wearing slacks, a sweater, and a black cashmere coat, and looked casual and chic, with her hair pulled back in a sleek ponytail, and just a hint of makeup. She looked surprisingly normal and young, and there was no hint of the green *Wizard of Oz* face. She was carrying Oscar in a black Birkin bag. Since Josh hadn't gone home to change, he was still wearing the same Metallica T-shirt, his battered leather biker's jacket, and torn jeans. He could see now why his outfit was inappropriate compared to how she looked. He was startled by how beautiful she was without the green face, and she looked surprisingly young.

"I'm sorry," he said softly, "I'll wear decent clothes tomorrow. They didn't tell me what you'd want me to do."

"It's all right," she said more calmly. "You can stay in the car. I have to pick up something I ordered at Hermès, look at something at Chanel, and get some things to send to Mr. West in England that he forgot to buy before he left, some special skin creams and shampoo. And I want to get a book to send to my daughter," she explained, as she led him to the garage, where he saw an elegant black Rolls, a black Range Rover, and a navy blue Bentley sports car. She headed to the Bentley and handed him the keys. "I assume you can drive a car too."

Josh broke into a broad smile. "I see your point. I'd look like I stole it if you weren't in the car with me." She laughed, and looked even prettier, much to his surprise.

"You're lucky the police didn't shoot you." She got into the passenger seat, and he slid behind the wheel and turned the car on, as the garage door opened and they headed out. She told him to go to Rodeo Drive first. These were the kind of errands he expected her to do. She was a star. And she looked very attractive dressed to go out.

"Is your daughter in college?" he asked her, and she smiled again.

"No, she's a plastic surgeon in New York." He was startled. She didn't look old enough to have a daughter that age.

"That's impressive." He wondered if she had worked on her mother's face. Ardith looked considerably younger than she was.

"What kind of actor are you?" she asked him, as they drove to Beverly Hills from Bel Air.

"An out-of-work actor," he said ruefully. "I've done a lot of sci-fi and horror movies that you'll never see."

"I did a horror movie once when I was twenty-two," Ardith said with a grin. "I was hoarse for weeks afterward, I had to scream so much. Then my husband discovered me and turned things around. He got me a decent agent, which made a big difference. Do you have an agent?"

"Yes. He doesn't know my name," Josh said.

"Have you studied?"

"Yes. I've changed directions a few times. I studied voice and piano at Juilliard. My mother was a piano teacher. My father wanted me to study physics and chemistry, which I hated. He was a professor at MIT. After Juilliard, I studied film at USC, and wanted to be a director, and eventually, when I was about thirty, I fell in love with acting, and I've been waiting on tables ever since. I keep hoping my ship will come in. It hasn't so far, but I'm not ready to give up yet," he said, and she nodded.

"That's what it takes. You just have to keep at it until you break down the door." She frowned then as she looked at him. "How old are you?" She guessed him to be in his late twenties or early thirties at most.

"Forty-one. I figure I'm due for a huge hit when I'm ninety. I can do mature parts then," he said with a lopsided grin.

"You look about twelve," she said, smiling too. "Or maybe thirty. You don't look forty-one."

"They have me playing all the way down to early twenties. I'll play anything, vampires, aliens, serial killers."

"Maybe you need to be more selective," she said seriously. "Don't be so obliging. If you're Juilliard-trained and did graduate work at USC, you have the credentials. You don't have to take all the crap they throw at you. Tell your agent you don't want those parts anymore."

"Then I'll get no work at all. I can't afford to be difficult," he said.

"Yes, you can, if you're any good. Are you a decent actor?" she asked him sincerely, looking him over.

"I like to think so, if I got a decent part."

"Why didn't you pursue singing, if you're Juilliard-trained?" She was curious about him now. He had an interesting background and seemed intelligent.

"I never loved it. It was my mother's dream for me. Acting is my passion. I'm willing to wait for the right part." She nodded, thinking about it, as they reached Rodeo Drive and he parked across the street from Hermès and Chanel.

"I won't be long," she said easily, and took Oscar out of her bag and dumped him in Josh's lap. "I'll leave him with you. He gets bored in stores."

"So do I," Josh said, looking suspicious of the dog.

"He'll be fine," she said, and hopped out of the car. She was halfway across the street when Oscar bared his fangs at Josh again.

"Don't start, or I'll leave you at the groomer for a week till you behave. We're stuck with each other, so don't give me any shit," he said firmly. Oscar jumped into the passenger seat, ignored Josh, and watched out the window for Ardith to return, but at least he had stopped snarling and showing his teeth. He and Josh politely paid no attention to each other, and Josh admired the beautiful car he was driving. He thought about the things Ardith had said to him about acting. He saw a whole other side of her when she did. She had seemed crazy to him that morning, and now she seemed like a decent human being and he had enjoyed talking to her. She was an odd contradiction of elements. He knew she was a star, but she didn't act like one. She acted more like a normal woman, doing errands, and not like the legend she was. She didn't appear to be impressed with herself, which surprised him, given who she was.

She came back nearly an hour later with two enormous shopping bags from Hermès and Chanel. From there, they went to the bookstore for her daughter, and the pharmacy for Bill. She was in good spirits by the end of the day and let Josh leave at four-thirty.

"I'm sorry about my arrival this morning. Thanks for not having me put in jail." He grinned. "I'll come dressed for work tomorrow, and I'll leave my Harley at home."

"That would be nice," she said with a smile, "and I won't hit the panic button. Sorry about that. We got off to a bad start."

"And I'm sorry they didn't send you a woman."

"That's okay," she said easily, as she gave Oscar his dinner before Josh left.

"So long, Oscar, see you tomorrow," Josh said easily, and Oscar turned to growl at him before he left, then went back to his dinner.

A few minutes later, she heard Josh roar away on the Harley and wondered what his life was like as a starving actor. He was tenacious if he was still trying to make it after ten years of sci-fi and horror movies. That couldn't be a lot of fun, and now he was stuck being an errand boy for her for two months. He didn't seem to have a wife and kids at forty-one, or at least he hadn't mentioned them if he did. She got the feeling that he was one of those dedicated actors who just wouldn't let go. She wondered if he had talent and was any good. He must have had musical talent at least to have graduated from Juilliard. He was an interesting guy, even if she had mistaken him for an axe murderer that morning. But he had looked like one to her.

Josh was thinking about Ardith when he got home, and the advice she had given him about not giving up. He wondered if she was right. How many more sci-fi movies could he do, or bad horror movies? He wanted a decent part so he could show that he could act, but had never gotten one. He was waiting for his big break, and now he was an errand boy. He wondered if his father had been right, and acting was a waste of time. Both his parents were gone now. They had had him late in life, and at least they hadn't had to see him starving and living hand-to-mouth, never in a decent movie. If he had to, he could have been a piano teacher, or played in some hotel bar, but the thought of it depressed him. He wanted to be an actor, not a piano teacher like his mother. He had grown up as an only child in Boston, had gone to New York to attend Juilliard, and had never gone back to Boston. Both his parents had died when he was at USC in graduate school, so he had stayed in L.A. and never moved back east again. But so far, his perseverance hadn't paid off, and he wondered if it ever would. He had almost gotten married a couple of times, but his acting career meant more to him, and he wasn't willing to take some boring ordinary job so he could support a wife and kids. At forty-one, he doubted that he'd ever marry now. Marriage wasn't high on his list, and his career was still more important to him. He hadn't had a girlfriend in a year.

He went to the gym after work and had a good workout, and when he got home, he sat down in his sparsely decorated apartment with furniture from Goodwill and lit a joint. He thought about how well Ardith Law lived, and how beautiful her home was, and wondered if that would ever happen to him. It didn't seem like it, but he didn't care if he lived in a tent on the street or in a cave, as long as he got a good part in a decent movie. He could taste it, he wanted it so badly, and he still wanted to prove his parents wrong that he was wasting his time, even though they'd never see it if he made it one day. Without realizing it, Ardith had rekindled his dreams that afternoon and given him hope again, and he was grateful to her. Even though the job was menial, he was excited about going to work the next day, although he couldn't ride his Harley and had to dress like a nerd for her. Maybe her advice was worth making the sacrifice. Maybe just being around her would bring him luck.

Ardith called Morgan that night, after Josh left on his Harley. She had to call early, because Morgan went to bed by eight or nine o'clock, and got up at five A.M., so she could do her surgeries early. On the days she wasn't operating, she went to the gym at five, before the office. Like her mother, she was an extremely disciplined person, and with New York being three hours later, Ardith always had to remind herself to call Morgan early on California time, before she went to bed. No matter what hour Ardith called, Morgan always sounded harassed and less than thrilled to hear from her mother. They both had to struggle to find safe subjects, so they wouldn't irritate each other.

"Did the assistant they promised you show up?" Morgan asked her.

"Yes," Ardith said noncommittally.

"How was she?"

"She was a man. He looked like a serial killer or a biker, I hit my panic button, and the police showed up," Ardith said, and Morgan laughed.

"That must have been fun. Did you have him arrested or just killed?"

"I explained that it was a misunderstanding, but they had him facedown on the ground before that, with their guns drawn."

"Now that's what I call a warm welcome," Morgan said, still laughing at her. "Did he quit?" Sometimes her mother amused her, and they both enjoyed a good chuckle. It was something at least.

"Not yet, but maybe he will. He's an out-of-work actor, desperate for work. I feel kind of guilty using him as an errand boy. He's a bright guy. He graduated from Juilliard, has a master's in film from USC. I don't know if he can act, but his credentials are impressive."

"Has he been in any decent movies?"

"Apparently not," Ardith said.

"Is he cute?" Morgan asked, amused.

"I don't know. I suppose he's decent-looking when he cleans up and isn't wearing his biker/serial killer look. Benicia and I thought he was going to break into the house, which is why I hit the panic button. He mostly just seems like a nice guy when you talk to him. He drove me around to do my errands today. He's terrified of Oscar, which is a little weird." Ardith grinned.

"Well, at least he can help you while Bill is gone. Maybe it's not so bad that he's a guy."

"I guess so, although I don't really need much help. Benicia and I manage just fine, unless he wants to do heavy stuff around the house, but he's not here for that. They only gave me someone to humor Bill."

"Well, it's still not a bad idea, if he's a decent person."

"What about you? What are you up to right now?" her mother asked her, and Morgan sighed.

"Working double time this week, while one of the senior partners is away at a convention in Korea. I'm seeing all his patients, and my own. It was a long day today and will be all week. But he has some interesting patients, so I don't mind," she said, but Ardith could hear that she was tired. Morgan worked too hard, but she enjoyed it. There was never a doubt in her mind that medical school had been the right choice for her.

Ardith went to bed that night thinking about her daughter and how different their interests were, although their work ethic was similar. And Ardith was missing Bill, but it was the wrong time to call him in England. With an eight-hour time difference, he would be asleep. She realized when he was away that even though she enjoyed having time to herself, after living with him for ten years he was a fixture in her life, and her days seemed empty when he wasn't around.

In the end, she waited until later, so she could reach him before his early morning studio call for hair and makeup. He was happy to hear from her. He sounded great, loved the cast, and was enjoying making the movie. She had read the script and he had a good part. He told Ardith all about it, and she wished she was working too. She wasn't jealous of him. She was happy for him, but she was ready to go back to work. She just had to find the right property, with a role for her that would be a perfect fit. She never settled for less.

She smiled before she fell asleep, thinking of how strong and young Bill sounded when he was working. It was just what he needed instead of following her around between films, but that was what he did when he wasn't working on a movie. Sometimes she felt guilty, but his constant close attention made her feel claustrophobic at times. It was oppressive, and she liked having time to herself, to think, to read, to digest what she'd read, sometimes to go back and read the book again. She needed space, which he didn't always give her, but in exchange, she had companionship, which she had missed when she was alone. What they had was more married than her marriage had been. She was an independent woman who didn't need constant companionship, which was something Bill never understood, and his feelings were hurt if she didn't want to be with him and needed time alone, no matter how often she explained it to him. A need for solitude and introspection just wasn't in his DNA. Bill wasn't a deep thinker, but he was a good person, and she was happy for him when she heard him sounding so pleased with the movie. She was going to visit him in England in a few weeks. There were friends she wanted to see there too, and a director or two she wanted to meet with to discuss future projects, and whatever they were working on at the moment.

When Josh showed up for work the next day, he was properly dressed and looked like a grown-up. This time she smiled when he rang the doorbell. He looked handsome and young, but not like a juvenile delinquent as he had the day before. He had even trimmed his hair himself and shaved before he came to work. He was wearing clean, pressed jeans, a white shirt, a tweed jacket he said he had gotten at a vintage store, and running shoes. He looked like a real assistant as she handed him a cup of coffee from the espresso machine, and he thanked her. He still didn't look his age, but he no longer looked twenty-five either.

"Thank you, you look lovely," she complimented him. He was handsome, and the time he spent at the gym had given him broad shoulders and a powerful build. He had a perfect body, and on looks alone, she thought he should have been getting better parts, if he was even a halfway decent actor. She suspected that his lack of work was due to a lazy agent, and was thinking of sending him to her own, if he proved worthy after he worked for her for a while. There was no rush—she had two months to get to know him and to get a sense of whether he was as serious as he said about his acting career. She suspected that he was, and she liked helping young unknown actors get ahead if they had talent and drive. She had a feeling that he had both.

In the meantime, she had him help her uncrate a painting she had bought at auction in New York. It was a beautiful French painting of a mother and child by a little-known Impressionist artist. It reminded her of Morgan when she was a little girl, and Josh was moved when he saw it. He helped Ardith pick the right place to hang it, put it on the wall for her, and then helped her light it. He was flattered when she asked his advice. They moved a few other paintings around to make room for it and found the right places for them too.

He took some packages to FedEx for her, brought back a list of things she needed from the hardware store, and helped her put an additional rack in Bill's closet, which she had wanted to do for ages and he wouldn't let her. The day ended in ignominy when she had Josh take Oscar to the groomer and pick him up, but for once the dog didn't snarl at him. He sat quietly in his special car seat and looked out the window. Looking at him made Josh smile, and then laugh out loud. Two days before he had looked like a biker, could go to the gym when he wanted, and was riding his Harley. Now he was alternately driving a Bentley and a Range Rover, and chauffeuring a toy poodle around. The dog was not part of the macho image he had of himself, but he was part of the job, along with hanging expensive paintings and riding around with the most famous movie star in the world. It was a lot to absorb in a short time. He liked the way people talked to him when he was properly dressed, as she required. He realized that she had a point. People didn't look at him the same way in a Metallica T-shirt and torn biker jeans as they did when he was wearing a sports jacket and a clean collared shirt.

He was intrigued by the way she talked about Bill occasionally, with tenderness and respect. He had a suspicion that the relationship wasn't passionate, but she obviously cared about him a great deal, and was genuinely happy that he was enjoying work on the movie in England. She wanted the best for Bill, and she obviously loved him, even though he was almost old enough to be her father.

She had mentioned to Josh on one of their errands that both of her parents were dead, when he said that his were. She said that hers had never approved of her acting career either. It had been her life-long dream, and she had come to L.A. right after high school from a small farming community in northern California. She had grown up on a farm, and she said her parents were devastated when she left to pursue her acting career and were vehemently opposed to it. Josh was stunned. She didn't look like any farm girl he knew. She said that John Walker had discovered her at an audition and eventually made her a star. And like Josh, she had worked as a waitress before that, to pay her rent. Her parents were even more opposed when she told them that she and John were getting married. She said her family thought he was exploiting her, which she realized later was probably true. But in the end, it benefited them both when she became a star.

She didn't tell Josh that she discovered later that John had cheated on her constantly, always looking for a younger, newer star, like the girl he had died with in the helicopter crash. He only got caught that time because they were killed together, and she found their letters in his desk drawer. She also found out over time that there had been many others like her. But Ardith was by far the biggest star he had ever made. And even if he had exploited her, it had been a fair exchange. She had had a forty-year career as a Hollywood legend thanks to him. She thought it was worth it now, even if he had broken her heart thirty years before.

It had been hard giving Morgan a fair image of her father, because Ardith had been angry at him for so long and hadn't forgiven him. But Morgan had created her own version that suited her needs for a fantasy father while she grew up. She knew the rumors and stories of his indiscretions. They were public knowledge after he died. He had been a legendary ladies' man. But somehow in spite of that she had invented a father who matched up to her dreams, which passed for memories now. It was a subject she and Ardith never discussed because their views about John Walker were so divergent and diametrically opposed. The truth about her father was still too hard for Morgan to accept, even now. Morgan had created the imaginary father who met her needs growing up, and she still clung to it. It was easier to blame her mother now for what she had lacked, rather than the man who was no longer there.

Josh was intrigued by what Ardith said about her family and her daughter, about Bill, about acting, about life. She didn't share with him her history with her late husband. She didn't know him well enough. She was a deep, sensitive woman, with profound ideas, which he realized now was why she was a great actress, because of what she brought of herself to the roles, not what they gave her. It was a lesson to him that he knew he would remember long after the two months he spent in her employ. He realized now that being hired as her errand boy, as a courtesy to Bill West, had been a serendipitous gift in his life. Josh hardly knew Ardith, but he already realized what a remarkable person she was. She wasn't always easy, but she was unusual and deep, and a good person. He wondered if her daughter understood that, or if Bill West appreciated it. It intrigued Josh too that she had never gone to college, but was very knowledgeable on many subjects, intelligent and extremely well read.

After only a few days riding around in a car with her, performing menial tasks together, he had a growing respect for her. It was like a plant being watered, and it grew each day. He felt like more of a grown-up with her than he ever had before. She expected it of him, just as she expected him to dress properly when he went out with her, and he felt better for it. She made him rise to the occasion and didn't cut him a pass because it was easier. She tried to explain to him that acting was like that. You could never give yourself a pass to take a shortcut. The long way around was always richer and brought with it more rewards. It was something he had never thought of before.

Along with the respect he felt as he got to know her came an urge to shield her and protect her from the people who would take advantage of her, or criticize and exploit her, and he realized now that there were many. It went with the territory of who she was. With fame, she had become an easy target for the greedy, the unkind, the jealous, and the unfair. And he realized that he was guilty of it himself, with all the unpleasant things he had assumed about her before they met, none of which had proven to be true so far. He could see a tendency to be a diva from time to time, if someone seriously irritated her, but he found that he could tease her out of it and make her laugh. She had a good sense of humor and was willing to laugh at herself.

"Sometimes I act like a spoiled brat," she confessed sheepishly.

"You aren't, though," Josh said thoughtfully, enjoying learning about her, and touched that she was so open with him. She was an honest person, even about her weaknesses and quirks. "I expected you to be very spoiled, and you're not."

"I'm usually only a brat when I'm very tired. Bill just ignores it when I misbehave. You called me on it in the hardware store yesterday when I was short with the salesman. I was being Ms. Law then. It's not a card I usually play." Josh had given her a look that brought her up short, caught her attention, and made her laugh.

"I thought you might slug me, but I took the chance," he said, and she laughed.

"You were right. You know, it's fun having you as an assistant. It's too bad you're probably a very good actor and you don't want to be an assistant forever." He made everything easier for her, and she liked talking to him.

"You make it very tempting." He smiled. He liked working for her, which was a surprise.

"You know, everything you learn in life you can apply to your acting. In fact, you have to, if you want to grow and improve." Listening to her, Josh realized that he hadn't pushed himself in a long time. He had been diligent about looking for work, but he hadn't tried to grow as a person in order to bring something more to the roles he tried out for, because he had been offered such lousy parts. But Ardith pointed out that even a lousy part could be improved if you put more of yourself into it. It was why she was a goddess of the screen, and he knew he was a mere mortal compared to her and always would be. Few actors or actresses had her stature or her gift. Even knowing her for a short time was an honor. He wanted to soak up everything she said to him in the next two months and remember it forever. And this was only the beginning. Every day was a rich experience with her and a life lesson. She seemed to have no idea how powerful her words were.

By the end of his first week with Ardith, Josh was deeply grateful that by some miracle he had gotten the job, and he laughed now at how he had dreaded it before he knew her. He couldn't wait to get to work every day and spend hours talking to her. At other times he could see that she needed to be alone, and he quietly withdrew and left her in peace to think or dream. He had never felt as attuned to another human being, or met a woman he liked and respected as much. She was nothing he had expected, and every day with her was a gift.

Chapter 3

The week had seemed long to Morgan in New York, covering for her senior partner, seeing his patients as well as her own. She had follow-up patients after their recent face-lifts. Two of them were thrilled with the results, and the third one less so, but Morgan assured her that it would settle in time, and look more natural in a few months. Some patients healed faster than others. She administered Botox shots to a number of her partner's regular patients, and saw a child with a severe burn on her arm, who was her own patient. There were going to be a number of skin grafts and surgeries, but so far the child was doing well. Morgan loved treating her. She loved the work she did with children, although she had no great desire for children of her own. Her life was full enough as it was, and she found her medical practice to be enormously rewarding.

She loved the group of doctors she worked with. They had a beautiful office and small surgery center adjacent to NewYork-Presbyterian Hospital, where they operated as well on more serious cases. She saw that her last patient of the day on Friday was a name she recognized. He was her partner's patient, a well-known TV anchor and correspondent on an important news show. He had been injured six months before in a hotel bombing in New Delhi, where he had been covering a story. He had sustained a deep gash on his cheek and had undergone several surgeries to repair it. He was scheduled for a routine check of his most recent surgery, which had been very successful. The senior partner did magnificent work. Morgan had learned a lot from him, and she admired the recent results again when she examined the patient post-surgery. His name was Ben Ryan, and he was surprised when he found Morgan waiting to examine him, and not his good friend who had performed the surgery.

"Andy is in Seoul," she explained, and Ben smiled as soon as he saw Morgan. She was a tall, beautiful blonde, whose looks were reminiscent of her mother's, although she was even taller and had a model's figure. Ben was tall as well and had a weakness for beautiful women, although Morgan was older than the women he usually went out with. But his attraction to the opposite sex, and appreciation of them, encompassed all ages. She had a sleek, elegant, sophisticated style. She was wearing a beige skirt and cashmere sweater the same color under her white lab coat, and high heels, which made her even taller. She had ice blue eyes, long straight blond hair, and a kind expression in her eyes when talking to her patients.

"Why has Andy been hiding you from me?" Ben Ryan said with a broad smile when he walked into her office.

"I think you two are old friends if I'm not mistaken," she said warmly.

"That's true. We went to Harvard together. But that's still no excuse." In the course of his banter, she examined the scar, which was greatly improved from what it had been, according to the photographs in his file, and he had possibly one more surgery scheduled in the coming months, depending on how this one healed over time.

"No problems, no lumps, no pain, no redness?" she asked him.

"None. My face is still slightly numb, but it's better than it was. Andy is a master at what he does. It was a mess when it first happened. You can hardly see it now, and I can cover it with makeup when I'm on camera."

Since he had gone to college with her partner, she guessed that Ryan was around sixty-three years old without checking his chart, although he didn't look it. He had a strong, well-toned, athletic body and a young face, with dark brown eyes and dark hair with gray at the temples. He was a strikingly handsome man, easily one of the best-looking men in TV news. She didn't know much of his personal history and didn't need to. The examination was routine and was over quickly. Morgan was going to a dinner party that night, given by a friend she had gone to medical school with, and hadn't seen in several months. She had little time for social life with her heavy schedule, and her dating life was sporadic for the same reason.

She'd had one serious romance in college, with what she referred to as another "Hollywood brat," the son of a famous actor, who had the same complaints she did about parents they never saw and who were always either on location or too busy to do the things that "normal" parents did. She would have married him if they'd both been older, but by the time they were, she was up to her ears in med school, and he got a young actress pregnant and married her instead. He had been married twice since, at thirty-eight, and she only got

Christmas cards from him, with photos of his five children. His children were as beautiful as the three women he had married, and he was a well-known director now himself, still living in L.A.

Morgan had fled California as soon as she went to college at Yale for undergraduate, then med school at NYU, and never moved back west. She loved her life in New York, and the practice she joined after her residency. She was an inveterate New Yorker now, and still had the same distaste for the Hollywood scene she'd had since her childhood, the same complaints about her mother, and ongoing resentments that had never entirely faded and flared up frequently.

Ben Ryan was curious about her. She was friendly but a little cool, and unlike most women he met, particularly those closer to his age, she made no attempt to flirt, and didn't respond when he did. He always found resistance of that kind appealing, like catnip. He could never resist a woman who didn't leap into his arms or appear to want him. Morgan maintained a professional demeanor with all her patients and was only warmer with children. With adults, she kept a cool, professional exterior that was strictly business. Most of Ben's conquests were easy, and he didn't have to work hard for them. He loved it when he did. Morgan reminded him to make another appointment in six weeks to see her partner, his old friend, for another routine check to decide about his next surgery, if he needed one.

She was making a note in his chart, at her desk, five minutes later when he called her. The receptionist put the call through.

"Did I forget something?" she asked, flustered for a moment when she took the call. The receptionist knew him because of his friendship with the senior partner.

"No, I did," he said, in a deep sexy voice. "I forgot to ask you to dinner. I was so bowled over when I met you that you had me in a daze the whole time you examined me," he said, and she laughed, caught off guard by what he said. She hadn't expected it, he was very direct. "I don't suppose you're free tonight? I'm not sure I can wait any longer. You're a dangerous woman, Dr. Walker," he said, and she laughed, embarrassed, not sure what to say. He was a very attractive man, but he was a friend of her senior partner, and she didn't think it would be wise to go out with him. She had never gone out with a patient before, although she had dated several doctors, but had never fallen in love with any of them. She had escaped what she considered the marital trap. She was totally focused on her career.

After graduation, Morgan had wanted to establish her career solidly, unencumbered by marriage. And the men who were serious about her didn't want to wait. They wanted a wife and babies, and she didn't want to get married. She had never met any man she wanted to marry. She was cautious about who she went out with and made it clear that her career was her priority. She was not unlike her mother in that way, and she had never dated a man Ben Ryan's age. He was a year older than her mother, which seemed like too wide an age gap to her. In spite of his youthful looks and style, he was twenty-five years older than Morgan.

"This may sound crazy to you, or like a line," Ben said to her, "but I knew the minute I met you that you're someone very special. I've only said that once or twice in my life, and I was right each time, and I know I am now. Are you free tonight?"

"No," she said, hesitating. "I'm going to a dinner party, which is rare for me. I get up very early. I perform my surgeries in the morning, and I need to be fresh and well rested when I do."

"I can tell you're very serious about your practice, or Andy wouldn't have you as a partner," Ben said.

"I don't think he'd like me going out with one of his patients," Morgan said simply. "It's never come up before." They had no official policy about it, but it seemed unprofessional to her.

"He's a sensible guy. I can have a talk with him if that would make you more comfortable," Ben offered.

"I'd rather you didn't," she said. "Maybe what happens after work hours doesn't concern him, if we're discreet about it." She was wavering. She was sorely tempted to see Ben Ryan again and flattered by his attention. She thought his news coverage was brilliant, and many of the men she met bored her, even fellow physicians. It would be nice not to be telling medical war stories on a date. While other surgeons bragged about their accomplishments, she was modest about her own, and the idea of an evening with a man out of the medical field was very appealing. She tried to justify it to herself as she listened to his deep mellifluous voice. There was a fluidity to it, and something very sensual.

"Tomorrow then?" he asked her, pressing the point home toward a victory. He could tell that she had weakened when she asked him to be discreet. He didn't get many refusals, but she might think him too old. He didn't know how old she was but guessed her to be somewhere in her mid-to-late thirties, given her position and obvious experience.

"All right," she said cautiously.

"You've just made me a very happy man. Shall I pick you up at eight o'clock? Does that work for you?"

"It's perfect. I'm not on call tomorrow. I've been on call all week for emergencies, since Andy's been away. He's due back tonight, so I'm off this weekend."

"That's excellent. Where do you live?" Morgan had an apartment in the East Sixties, not far from the hospital, which was convenient, in a modern building, with a view of the East River. She gave him the address and he promised to be there. As soon as she hung up, she had a moment of regret, and wondered if her senior partner would be angry if he found out, but there was no reason why he should hear of it, and Ben had promised his discretion.

She thought about Ben all the way home, and was excited about the date, even if she felt guilty about it. He was so seductive and so direct and his attention was very flattering. He had enormous charisma. He was a very famous man, and incredibly bright. Her mother's fame didn't impress her, she was used to it, but Ben's did. He had a quick, sharp mind and was very intelligent and worldly.

She wore a new black dress for their date the following night. It was chic and subtly sexy. She put her blond hair in a bun, and added a black coat, and diamond stud earrings she had bought herself. Her heels were high, her skirt was short, and her legs looked terrific. None of it was lost on Ben when he picked her up, and he looked dazzled. He had a car and driver, and took her to Le Bernardin, one of the best French restaurants in New York. She had never been there but heard a lot about it from her partners. They had a very lucrative practice. The men Morgan occasionally dated took her to simpler, more casual places. She wasn't used to being wooed at the level Ben did. Dinner with him was sophisticated, glamorous, and exciting. He told her he had been married twice, the first time in his twenties. It had lasted for five years, he hadn't enjoyed the experience, and he had waited another twenty years to remarry. At fifty, he had married a thirty-year-old weather forecaster on his show. It had lasted a year and ended in a shockingly expensive divorce that was all over the tabloids, she vaguely remembered.

He had a thirty-five-year-old daughter from his first marriage who he said was an artist and a perennial student. She lived in Paris, was taking classes at the Louvre for the third time, and had gone to the Beaux-Arts before that, and she lived with a French boyfriend Ben said he didn't like much. He was a starving artist and Ben thought she could do better. He said he didn't see her often, and he had been traveling as a foreign correspondent for most of her childhood and had missed a lot of important moments. He regretted it now, but it was too late. At thirty-five, she was no longer eager to spend time with her father. "I missed the boat on that," he confessed to Morgan.

"And do you want more children, to make up for it?" she asked, curious about him. She wondered if her own father would have said the same things about her if he had lived. He had been gone most of the time too, and then he died.

"It's too late for me," he said simply. "I don't want children at my age, and I have my daughter. She's terrific, and I want to spend my time now with another grown-up, and not start all over again with a young wife and little kids. A lot of my friends do, but it's not for me. I don't know how they do it. What about you? Desperate for babies? Is that clock ticking?" She smiled and shook her head.

"I've never wanted children. A husband maybe someday, but not kids. It wouldn't be fair to them. My work is too important to me. My parents were busy, my father died when I was very young, and my mother was always traveling for her work. I know what that feels like, as a child, and I've never wanted to do that to someone else. Some people just shouldn't have children. I think I'm one of them. So was she," she said, and he looked relieved when she said it. He was constantly running into women who wanted marriage and babies, since he usually dated younger women. From thirty on, most of the women he met were ready to settle down, especially with a famous husband. But he had a habit of choosing women for their looks and personalities, not their depth. Morgan felt like just the right age to him, and the right woman. He listened raptly to her all night, and they were the last couple in the restaurant. He walked her home after that. It was a cold, clear night, and it was invigorating. Their eyes were bright and their faces chilled when they got to her building. It was late and they'd had a wonderful time and hadn't stopped talking all night.

"When can I see you again?" he asked her as he hugged her, and her doorman waited at a discreet distance.

"I have a heavy week next week, with a lot of surgeries. January is always a busy month, after the holidays."

"Next weekend?" he asked hopefully, and she nodded. He didn't kiss her. It was too soon, but their mutual desire was obvious and palpable. He was a dazzling man and would be easy to fall for. Morgan hadn't thought of their age difference all night and didn't care. Ben was infinitely more worldly, sophisticated, and intelligent than any man she'd ever gone out with. And he was just as impressed with her. He loved the fact that she wasn't desperate for a husband and babies, which was a big relief to him. He had told her clearly during dinner that his career had never been compatible with marriage. And she wasn't sure hers was either, although both of her partners were married. He had also admitted to her that he wanted to write a novel when he retired, but he had no plans to retire for the moment. He still had a heavy travel schedule and a demanding job. He was at the top of his career and intended to stay there for a long time. He was incredibly charismatic, and a star. Morgan could hardly wait to see him again. His lips had brushed her cheek when he left her, and she turned to wave as she went into her building. He was standing watching her with a schoolboy smile on his face, and then he got into the car he'd had follow them to her building. Ben was the most exciting man she had ever gone out with, and she loved the aura of sophistication about him. He thought Morgan was the most interesting woman he had met in years, and so beautiful it made his heart ache to look at her. They could both sense that something powerful had happened, and that without intending to, they had started something dangerous that night, like a forest fire that neither of them could control and didn't want to.

Ardith had a quiet night. She thought about Bill, but it was late to call him. She thought about Josh too, and how pleasant and easy it was to talk to him. They'd gotten a lot done that week, little projects that she had wanted to do for ages, that weren't worth hiring someone for, and that Bill would never help her with. He hated projects in the house, and she enjoyed them. Josh had gone on errands with her. He was good company and Oscar had finally stopped growling at him. They hadn't made friends yet, but Oscar was tolerating him, so at least he wasn't barking constantly when Josh showed up for work. Josh was turning out to be a real blessing. She got a lot done with him. He joked about being her cabana boy after a week of working for her. He admired how open, direct, honest, and straightforward she was, so that he had forgotten his earlier objections. Ardith was above all very human. And he was coming to understand the price she paid for fame.

She was surprisingly isolated and had to deal constantly with people's misconceptions about her. They were public tides she could never turn and just had to endure, which seemed unfair to him, but was the nature of fame.

In two weeks, she was flying to London to see Bill, and Josh would be off while she was away. Ardith had talked to Bill several times, and he said he was taking all his pills and feeling fine. He was enjoying the work, the cast and crew, and was in good spirits when she talked to him. He sounded lively, happy, and excited to be working. Being on a film was always good for him and rejuvenated him. He had asked about the assistant and was surprised it was a man, and she said it was working out well. And Bill was more interested in his movie.

She went to bed early and was in a deep sleep when the phone rang at one in the morning. She always answered it at night, in case it was Morgan and there was some unforeseen emergency. She groped for her cell phone next to her bed and held it to her ear, without putting her glasses on to see who was calling. She came awake at the sound of an unfamiliar voice at the other end. It was one of the producers in London on location with the cast, and she assumed he had calculated the time difference incorrectly. It was nine A.M. in London.

"Ms. Law?" he asked her, and she answered with her eyes closed.

49

"Yes." She glanced at the clock then, saw the time and sat up in bed. She was about to ask him if she could call him back in the morning, when she heard the tone of his voice, and came fully awake in an instant.

"I'm afraid I have some very bad news. Mr. West had a massive heart attack during the night and passed away in his sleep. The doctor assured us that he never woke up and didn't suffer. He died peacefully." Ardith didn't say a word for a moment, as the words sank in, like torpedoes hitting a submarine. She felt as though she was drowning the moment she heard them. There had been no way to cushion the bad news. The producer had to tell her the truth.

"That can't be. He didn't have a heart problem. He just had a checkup recently." She wanted him to tell her that it was a mistake, it wasn't true. But Bill was seventy-eight years old, and it had happened. She suddenly couldn't remember the name of the man she was talking to. "Who is this? Are you sure?"

"Peter Price, I'm the onsite producer. And I'm so very, very sorry. Bill was a wonderful person and we all loved working with him. And yes, I am sure. We called the emergency medical services as soon as we found him, and the medical examiner came immediately. Bill was already gone when someone went to check on him this morning—we tried to revive him, but he'd been dead for several hours. He didn't come to the set this morning and was late for hair and makeup. I'm so very, very sorry. We'll call the airline and the U.S. embassy today and make all the arrangements to send him home. There are formalities we must observe. I'll call you in a few hours when I know more. I wanted to let you know immediately, so you wouldn't hear it on the news. The media have already gotten hold of it. I'm sure it will be on all the news channels this morning."

"What do you need me to do? Should I come over?" she asked, feeling lost. She hadn't dealt with anyone dying since Morgan's father after the helicopter accident. This was a terrible déjà vu. And she knew that Bill was the last living member of his family, so Ardith would have to take care of everything. She felt dazed as she listened to Peter Price tell her about the red tape they'd have to get through in order to send Bill's body back to California. Ardith was a person who normally handled everything and balked at nothing. She had organized John's funeral perfectly, even with the scandal of the girl who'd been with him. But suddenly now, faced with the news of Bill's death, she felt helpless. But Bill was seventy-eight years old, and it had to happen someday. She just hadn't expected it so soon. She thought she'd have another ten years with him, but fate had other plans.

The producer tried to delicately remind her that it was a painless way to go and a blessing for Bill, even if hard for his loved ones. But Bill had none, except her. She had been listed as his next of kin, so they had called her. At times, she had thought of him diminishing slowly eventually, maybe being bedridden for a long time, and then dying. She had never expected it to happen this suddenly and this swiftly. One phone call and he was gone, a week after she'd last seen him. She hadn't had a chance to say goodbye and had no inkling of it. He had told her every day on the phone that he felt great. Was he lying to her, or did he really have no warning? And did it matter now anyway? He was gone, swept away on the tides of life, just as he had once been born into this world, and now his time was up.

Their twelve years of loving companionship were over. Just thinking about it, she had never felt so alone in her life. She kept reminding herself that he hadn't suffered. And maybe the producer was right. He'd been having fun on the set, enjoyed the camaraderie he had described to her, had entertained everyone, and told wonderful stories of his early days in Hollywood, and now it was over. He had gone to his eternal rest, and Ardith was alone again. She already knew that he had left all his earthly possessions to her. He had no money to speak of, and she didn't need anything from him, and never expected it. All she wanted now was another year or five or ten, and instead she had nothing. It was over. He was gone and he was never coming back, except for his remains, to be buried whenever they sent him for a funeral that all Hollywood would want to attend, just as they had John's, which she had had to organize in spite of the humiliation that was his final gift to her. She had never forgiven him for it. She had nothing to forgive Bill for. He had simply gone to sleep and never woken up. It was the way almost anyone would want to die, but she didn't want him to die at all. She wanted him to come home.

As she sat in bed after the call and thought about Bill's death, she was wracked by great gulping sobs, of sadness and loss, and grief that she hadn't been with him when it happened. And what was she going to do now without him? She wanted to call Morgan, but she didn't dare. She knew how busy Morgan was every day, and she didn't want to disturb her in the middle of the night. There was nothing Morgan could do for Bill or her mother. It was over, peacefully, swiftly, irrevocably. Bill West had left Ardith's life, as smoothly and quietly as he had once entered it. Without a sound, or a goodbye.

And Ardith would have to make her peace with it and learn to live without him. The age difference between them had caught up with them in the end, and she was alone again.

She sat in bed for the rest of the night, wide awake, alternately crying and just staring into space and thinking about him, the man he had been when they met, the one he had become with time, as he slowed down, and what he had meant to her. It all blended together now. A legend had died, a sweet man, an old-school gentleman, a beloved companion, and for better or worse, she had loved him as much as she was able, whatever their limitations. And an important chapter in her life was over now. She was on her own again.

Chapter 4

Ardith waited two hours after she heard the news. It was six A.M. in New York, and she called Morgan, knowing she would be on the way to the hospital by then to begin her surgeries, before her office hours later in the day. Morgan answered her phone as she walked to the hospital, and was surprised to see her mother's number. Despite old grievances and their differences, she was concerned. Her mother was still relatively young, but anything could happen medically and her mother never called her at that hour. It was three A.M. in L.A.

"Are you okay?" Morgan asked her.

There was a flicker of hesitation before Ardith answered, and a lump in her throat. "No . . . yes . . . I'm okay. Bill died in his sleep in London. They called me two hours ago to tell me." Morgan could hear that Ardith was crying, as she digested the news herself. She had never been close to Bill, but she knew that her mother loved him, and they had been inseparable for the past twelve years, even though they never married. Morgan didn't fully understand the relationship or why Ardith hadn't wanted to marry him. Ardith said she thought it unnecessary and it worked well enough as it was, although Bill had always said he would have preferred to be married, which seemed more respectable to him. Ardith didn't want to be more committed than she was. The legalities weren't important to her, since her only marriage had turned out to be a sham when John Walker cheated on her. She didn't want to run the risk of being cheated on again, although Morgan doubted that Bill West had ever betrayed her. And she knew that his absence would leave a huge void in her mother's life now.

"I'm so sorry," Morgan said in a shocked voice and stopped walking outside the hospital. Cell reception in the hospital was spotty. She hadn't expected this kind of news, and Bill had seemed in relatively good health for his age, despite all the medications he took, many of them preventative. He had had no serious conditions once he beat the prostate cancer. "What happened?"

"A massive heart attack. With no warning. He was feeling fine and having fun on the picture, and now he's gone. They say he died in his sleep and didn't suffer."

"I'm sure that's true," Morgan reassured her. "I'm so sorry. Do you have to go over?"

"The producers will take care of everything and send him home. There are some formalities. I have to plan the funeral." Ardith hated to ask her the next question, but she wanted to know. "Will you come home?" There was silence at Morgan's end for a moment.

"When? Now? I can't, Mom. I have surgeries scheduled all week. When do you think the funeral will be?"

"I don't know. I assume next week sometime. It will probably take this week to get him home."

"I'll come for the funeral. Just let me know when as soon as you can, but I can only stay for the day." Bill wasn't her father, or even her stepfather. He had been pleasant and polite to her, but never warm. He was her mother's companion and friend. This was Ardith's grief to deal with now, not hers. Morgan was acutely aware of it and didn't have the time to spend weeks or even days to comfort her mother. Her work schedule didn't allow it, and the nature of their relationship didn't encourage it either. Her mother would adjust without Bill in time. And Morgan thought Ardith had been spared years of possible nursing at the end. It was a mercy that he had gone so quickly and so simply. He could have become an enormous burden to her mother as he got older, and now he wouldn't. Ardith was free to pursue her life without him. Morgan thought it was for the best this way, although she didn't say it to her mother. "I'm sorry, Mom. Let me know if there's anything I can do from here," which they both knew there wouldn't be. All Morgan could do now was offer comfort to her mother. She didn't have the time, the nature, or the desire to fill the void in her mother's life. They had been too separate and too distant for too long. Ardith was reminded yet again that she would forever pay the price of what she hadn't been able to provide Morgan when she was a child.

"I understand," Ardith said, sounding shaken. She had never felt as vulnerable as she did now. When John Walker died, she had been young. Bill dying now made her face her own mortality too, an unpleasant thought, even if he had been sixteen years older. But one day, sooner or later, something similar would happen to her. She had lost several friends to cancer in the last few years, but there had been time with them to adjust to the loss, and prepare for it. With Bill, there was no warning. He was suddenly and instantly gone.

Morgan looked at her watch as she stood outside the hospital. "I have to go, Mom. I have to check my patients, and I'm due in surgery in ten minutes. I can't be late. I'll call you when I get to the office this afternoon. One of them is a long surgery this morning." She was doing a face-lift.

"It's okay, don't worry. I'll be fine. And Morgan . . . I love you," Ardith said in a tender voice.

"I love you too, Mom. And I'm sorry about Bill. I know how much he meant to you." Ardith had taken good care of him and loved him to the best of her abilities. There had always seemed to be something lacking in it to Morgan, maybe because they weren't married, so despite the longevity of their relationship, she had never taken it too seriously. She wondered if she'd been wrong, and if it had been a deeper love than she thought, as she and her mother hung up and she hurried into the hospital and took the elevator up to the surgical floor. Her mother was clearly deeply shaken by the loss, but sudden death was always shocking, even if a mercy in the end. Morgan turned her mind to her patients then, changed into scrubs, and went to visit two of them before she started. They were already sedated, and she went to scrub for the surgeries that would occupy her all morning. However upset she was now, Morgan knew her mother would be fine. Ardith was a strong woman and had come through worse before. Morgan wasn't worried about her, even if she knew she would be sad for a time, which was normal. Morgan wasn't a nurturer, particularly with her mother.

Ardith sat in her bed, thinking for a while, after she spoke to Morgan. She wasn't surprised by anything her daughter said. She was a doctor, and death wasn't unfamiliar to her. And even though in relatively good health, Bill wasn't young. As one of her friends said recently, it was both the blessing and the curse of being with older men. Sooner or later they died, while you were still young. The friend who had said it already had a new man in her life six months after her husband had died. Ardith knew that wouldn't happen to her. She had always thought that whenever Bill died, she would prefer to stay alone, to work harder than she was working now if she found good parts, press on in her career again, travel, visit Morgan in New York, and live free from the complications of a relationship where she had to take care of someone who would eventually be in failing health. Even if she found a man her own age now, it would require a level of commitment she was no longer prepared to give. But she hadn't expected to be freed from her responsibilities so soon.

She went to the kitchen, made herself a cup of coffee, and went back to bed, thinking of Bill and all she had to do. She stayed close to the phone, waiting for news from London. She turned on the TV to see the morning news and was shocked to see a very handsome younger photo of Bill fill the screen. The newscasters reported on his death in London the night before and mentioned the high points of his career and some of his major films. They mentioned his two brief marriages to well-known actresses many years before, showed a photo of him with Ardith at the Academy Awards when she received her second Oscar, and said they had been constant companions for the past decade but weren't married. They said he had no children, that his death would be mourned in the film industry, that he would long be remembered by fans, and that funeral arrangements had not yet been made since he had died abroad only hours before. And then they moved on to the next story.

It seemed little to say about a man who had been in the public eye for so long and had been admired by fans all around the world. As she listened, Ardith wondered if it was enough for a life of nearly eighty years. Was that really all there was? Over a hundred films, no children, no wife in the end. But she knew it had been enough for Bill. He had been satisfied with the life he led, and never questioned himself the way she did. It was one of the major differences between them. Ardith always dug deeper and questioned herself. Bill was always content with how things were, and stayed on the surface. He was happier as a result, and now it was over. She sat quietly thinking about him. She heard Benicia moving around in the kitchen, she didn't want to see her yet. Ardith knew that Benicia watched morning TV and was sure she had already seen the news. She stayed in bed until she heard Josh arrive at nine. She put on a bathrobe and went to meet him in the kitchen, while Benicia vacuumed the living room.

Josh was neatly dressed and smiled when he saw her. She could see from the cheerful look on his face that he hadn't heard the news yet, and he seemed surprised when he saw her look so solemn.

"Are you okay?" he asked her cautiously. She looked pale and exhausted. She had been awake since Peter Price called her from London.

"Bill died last night, in his sleep in London," she said, and Josh looked shocked. Due to an odd quirk of fate, he found himself in their inner circle now, privy to the sorrows and joys of their lives, and inexorably part of them. It wasn't what he had expected or intended when he had been cast in the role of her "errand boy," as he called himself, during Bill's absence, and now he was one of them, and in one short week had come to care about them.

"Oh no! I'm so sorry," he said, moving toward her. She looked bereft, lost and alone, more than devastated. She had been caught off balance when she got the call. Now she was facing it squarely hours later, but deeply sad nonetheless. "What can I do to help you?" Josh said, as she sat down in a kitchen chair and looked up at him.

"I don't know yet. I'm going to have to do everything. He had no one."

"No kids?"

She shook her head, looking at Josh. "Just me. There's some red tape about bringing him home. The producers are dealing with it. After that, it's up to me. I want to write a decent obituary. I'll call his agent. He made a lot of movies. He was a good person," she said sadly. She felt guilty now that she hadn't loved him more than she did. She was faithful and devoted and attentive to him, but she knew that she didn't love him unquestioningly as he did her. He had loved her unconditionally. With Ardith, there were always deeper questions that had no answers, which was why her performances were so brilliant, because she always dug down for the hard questions and answers, in the roles she played as in life, and was always critical of herself and her performances and relationships with other humans. She had realized long since that she had never trusted another man after her husband. Her father had been a good man, but had died young too, and her mother had been a weak woman who had accepted everything at face value, which had given Ardith the role model of who she didn't want to be. And her parents had never understood or approved of her career as an actress. She had been a stranger in their midst since her childhood. And there had never been a man who truly understood her, not even Bill, who accepted her as she was without digging deeper, but didn't really understand her either. She had no illusions about that, even now.

Josh made himself a cup of coffee and sat down at the kitchen table with her. Ardith didn't object, it was comforting to have him there even though she barely knew him. But he was bright and caring. Benicia came in and looked like she'd been crying, told Ardith how sorry she was, they hugged, and then Benicia went to tidy Ardith's bedroom and left them alone.

"He always accepted me just as I was, even when I was bad or ill-tempered." Josh smiled. "He didn't care why I did what I did, he just accepted me and never punished me. Everyone else in my life always did. They kept score, just like Morgan does. Bill never did. He was such a good person. He was uncomplicated, which is why it worked for so long." She looked mournfully at Josh, who didn't comment. He just let her talk. He knew she needed to, to work through what had happened. "What do I do with his things now? There's no one to give them to," she said, as though that mattered, but it was something to keep her mind busy.

"There must be some kind of museum for the film industry that would be happy to have some of it," he suggested quietly, and she nodded, remembering the Hollywood Museum. "And I'll call his agent and get all the biographical material they have on him, and I can check the internet, so you can write the obit."

"Thank you," she said, grateful for his thoughts that would help her navigate her way through it.

He called the museum and Bill's agent and got all the pertinent information for her. He answered the phone for her all day, as the shocking news spread out into the world like water. Bill had been well liked and admired by his peers, and people were genuinely sad at the news of his passing. There was no one Ardith wanted to talk to, even among her friends. She needed to cope with her own emotions before she dealt with anyone else's, and dealing with the biographical material on Bill that Josh gathered for her gave her a safe place to take refuge. Facts were easier to deal with than feelings.

Josh stayed late that night, helping her organize the material for Bill's obituary. Like everything else she did, she wanted it to be perfect and accurate. Josh didn't want to leave her alone, and the obituary was a good excuse to keep an eye on her. He felt sorry for her but didn't let it show. He could see that she was coping with her own emotions and couldn't deal with anyone else's. Morgan called her once and the conversation was brief.

Ardith was still working on the obituary when he left that night, and she had a draft to show him in the morning when he arrived. It was beautifully written, and he only made one or two suggestions, which she thanked him for and incorporated in what she'd written.

Peter Price called her from London that afternoon. The ambassador had helped them with the inevitable red tape of an American citizen of Bill's celebrity dying abroad. His remains were to arrive on Friday, which allowed her to begin planning the funeral. She wanted it to be as dignified and traditional as he was, an event that everyone would remember and that would pay suitable homage to him. It was the last thing she could do for him, and she was bearing the full expense herself. When she spoke to his agent, his bank, and his attorney, who confirmed that she was both the executor of Bill's estate and the only heir, she was shocked at how little money he had left. He lived from movie to movie and was counting on the current one to fill his coffers again, for however long it lasted. His estate would have to go through probate, which would take time, but in effect, he owned nothing of value and had no investments, and what money he had wouldn't have paid for the flowers at his funeral. She intended to pay for his final elegant farewell, worthy of the star he was, and Josh made an appointment for her with both a church and a funeral home the next day, so she could make the arrangements. He had instantly become more than an errand boy, and was a seriously useful assistant, who helped her do everything, and he rapidly understood that she was paying for everything, just as she had when Bill was alive. It had never been an issue between them, and she handled it with such grace that Bill had never felt humiliated by it.

The only shocking call Josh received was at his apartment the next morning. He was due to take Ardith to the funeral home, where she was arranging a viewing for Bill's friends and a public one for his fans. Josh was organizing security for it, and for her as well. An emotional event of this kind brought the crazies out, the police had warned him, and Josh wanted to make sure that Ardith was protected, since there was no one else to think of that now. She was thinking of Bill and what was due him, and Josh was focused on her.

The call he got that morning was from the producer of Bill's movie, who had hired Josh to work for Ardith as an assistant for two months as part of their deal with Bill West, as a courtesy to Bill and at his request, since he would be on location and unable to help her. Josh had considered it a jail sentence when they offered it to him initially.

"Well, you're off the hook," the producer told him on the phone.

"For what?" Josh's head was full of the funeral arrangements he was helping Ardith with, and nothing else. It had become his mission to help her, and he was relieved to be useful to her in a meaningful way. She was disoriented and shocked by Bill's sudden death.

"You can forget being Ardith Law's slave." There were six weeks left to run in the agreement, and Josh was being respectably paid and needed the money. It allowed him not to work as a waiter while he waited for another minor part in a movie to come through, so he could pay his rent. And even though he hadn't wanted the job at first, the money was good. "We spoke to our legal department this morning. The agreement was in a side letter to humor Bill West, it wasn't in his contract, but with his death, that part of the agreement is null and void, so you're done. I'm sure that's good news. She's probably a bitch to work for, and she has no claim on us. We had no agreement with her. So, it's over. You can give her notice as of today, or we can do it for you, if you want. You don't even have to go back. You're out. We figured you'd be thrilled."

Josh was silent for a moment, thinking of all the things he was doing for and with her, and knew his leaving would be yet another blow. She had no one else to help her. No assistant of her own, since she hadn't done a film in two years, and Morgan was uninvolved, too busy in New York to help her mother, and didn't seem inclined to.

She seemed to figure her mother had nothing else to do and could manage on her own.

"I'm helping her with the funeral arrangements," Josh said carefully, thinking about it as he said it. "I hate to leave her in the lurch."

"We're very sorry about Bill. He was a great guy, but Ardith Law isn't our problem. We don't owe her anything and she can afford to hire an assistant if she needs one. And we have a script we're just closing a deal on that we want to send you in the next few weeks."

"Another horror movie?" Josh asked in a flat voice, and the producer laughed.

"No, a good one this time. A part we think you'd be perfect for. We're going to send it to your agent. It's a strong supporting role in a dramatic film, with a great director." It was exactly what Josh wanted, but the timing was terrible. He didn't want to leave Ardith upset and alone. He had only worked for her for two weeks, but felt a loyalty to her now, and an attachment. He knew better than most people how vulnerable she was underneath the hard, confident exterior, which was only a front.

"And she's not a bitch, by the way. She's a decent woman."

"I'm happy to hear it. But you're done. We'll pay you through this week, and then the arrangement is canceled. We haven't told her yet, we were going to let her agent know, as a courtesy. We never had a deal with her, only with Bill, to provide her an assistant while he was on location."

"Don't tell her agent," Josh said firmly. "I'll take care of it, I'll give her notice today, and finish out the week."

"Fine. And we'll get that script to your agent as soon as we sign the deal. I think you're going to be very happy with it. This could be your big break."

"Thank you, I look forward to reading it," Josh said, distracted by what the producer had said. The money they were going to pay him for two weeks as her assistant would carry him for a while, and he could cover his rent with his savings. He didn't need much more than that at the moment, and if he had to, he could borrow money from a friend. He had before, and always paid them back. He sat staring into space after he hung up, figuring it out. There was no way he was going to leave her now, and she didn't need to know the arrangement was over. She was a good woman and he cared about her, and she'd had a hard blow with Bill's death and no one to support her through it. Working for her for the next six weeks, to finish out his time with her, was a gift he could give her. He was willing to work for the next six weeks with no pay, and she never had to know about it. It was something he could do for her. He had enough in his bank account now for two or three rent checks, which was all he needed. He didn't want to leave her to work as a waiter during the next six weeks he was supposed to work for her. She didn't need to lose him too, as her only helper and person to lean on. She could hire an assistant later if she needed one, as the producer said, but for now, he was going to do everything he could to help her and get her on the road to recovery after Bill's death. The script they said they wanted to send him sounded interesting, if it ever happened, but most of the promises they made and projects they told him about fell through and never materialized. He expected to go back to waiting on tables in six weeks. In the meantime, he was going to be fully available to Ardith to help her. She didn't need to know he was no longer being paid. He had been shocked when the producer called him to say that his time as her assistant was over. It was the last thing he expected, but it made sense in the circumstances. He had hated to hear the producer call Ardith a bitch. She wasn't. He was sure she could be tough when she needed to be, but she hadn't been a bitch to him, and if anything, he felt as though they were friends now, and he was not going to let her down in her hour of need.

He arrived on time to take her to the appointment at the funeral home, and to meet with the priest at the Church of the Good Shepherd in Beverly Hills afterward. She was clear, capable, and well organized with the arrangements she made. She was spending a fortune to provide Bill with a hero's funeral he would have been proud of, and she had absolutely no idea that Josh would be working for free now. It never dawned on her.

In a quiet moment over a cup of coffee when they got back to the house, he told her about the script the producer had promised to send, if it ever happened, and Ardith looked at him with interest.

"Show it to me when you get it," she said. "I'll tell you what I think of it. Half of what really matters in this business is picking the right scripts. A lot of actors overlook that and get enthused about the wrong things. The writing is key. I'm happy to take a look, if you want me to." He couldn't think of anything better.

"Thank you. Most of the projects they tell me about like that never happen, and I never hear from them again. We'll see if they even send it to me." He didn't sound optimistic. He'd been disappointed too many times.

"Just let me know if you get it." They went back to talking about the funeral then. They had made a lot of headway that morning. She had picked a beautiful photograph of Bill for the program, and the music she knew would be meaningful to him. There was going to be a notice in the *L.A. Times* of both the funeral and the public viewing, and Josh had lined up security and police protection. It was going to be a major event, and they expected several thousand fans and friends to attend. One of the longtime heroes and stars of old Hollywood was being put to rest with a hero's send-off. Ardith was paying more than adequate tribute to him, and she saw to every minute detail with Josh's help.

The funeral was set for the following Monday, with a full mass at the Church of the Good Shepherd. Bill's body was due back from London on Friday. Josh was going to meet the casket with her at the airport. He didn't want her facing that alone.

When Ardith called Morgan to tell her that afternoon, Morgan said that she was busy that weekend and couldn't come to L.A., but she would arrive on Sunday night, attend the funeral with her mother on Monday, and fly back to New York Monday evening. Ardith was holding a reception at the Hotel Bel-Air after the funeral, and Morgan said she couldn't attend that either and would have to leave after the church service and the burial at Hollywood Forever Cemetery, which was at least something. Josh thought that Morgan could have made more effort to be with her mother for all of it, but he didn't say anything, and Ardith didn't argue with her. Morgan always placed firm boundaries on her time with her mother, and Ardith accepted it, knowing that she had fallen short in her motherly duties in the past. Morgan had the upper hand with that, and had kept score and never let her mother forget it. At least she was coming. That was something, although she would have little time to offer her mother comfort and support. But Ardith would have friends there, her agent, Bill's friends, and the filmmakers they'd worked for, and Josh discreetly in the background. She would get through it, even without Morgan attending all of it. Josh thought it wasn't nice of Morgan, but he never said a word. And he admired Ardith for her restraint. In her shoes, he would have said more to Morgan, but Ardith knew better. Morgan gave as much of herself as she wanted, and never more, particularly to her mother. And Josh quietly observed it all.

Chapter 5

M eeting Bill's casket at LAX when it arrived from London was a sobering experience, which made Bill's death that much more real to Ardith and even to Josh, who had never met him and went to the airport with her. The funeral home sent a hearse to collect the casket with Bill's remains and take it to the funeral home to prepare him for the viewing on Sunday.

Ardith stood on the tarmac with a devastated look as they lowered the casket carefully on a hydraulic lift. The producers in London had sent Bill home in a simple pine box, and Ardith had selected a dignified-looking mahogany casket for the funeral and the viewing. She had spent a fortune on it, which was the nature of funerals in America. Josh had been horrified by what they charged her for every service, and for everything she needed. It was above all a lucrative business, which preyed on people at their most vulnerable time. And in the case of a star of Ardith's magnitude, they took advantage of every opportunity. Josh tried to help guide her through the rough currents which she was navigating, he thought, with surprising grace and patience. Several times, he would have lost his temper, but he didn't, for her sake, and Ardith was gracious and kind to everyone.

Watching the casket removed from the plane was upsetting, and she looked shaken and pale afterward when they left the airport to go home. The casket was on its way to the funeral home in the hearse by then, and she had signed all the necessary documents to acknowledge receipt of William West's remains for burial.

"Are you okay?" Josh asked her gently on the way back to Bel Air. She nodded, unable to speak for a minute as she wiped her eyes. Seeing Bill's casket had made it all more real to her. It wasn't about what flowers and what music, or a fancy casket. It was about bringing home the body of a man she had loved for twelve years, shared her life with, and shared her bed with for all of those years. A man she would never see again and who would never be part of her life again. However imperfect their relationship may have been, it had been human and real, as real as they were, and had carried them through a dozen years. She knew that she would miss him, once all the fanfare was over. That part of it didn't seem real to her yet, so the missing was not as acute as she suspected it would be later. For now, Josh was helping to keep her distracted with the arrangements, which were all-consuming.

"When does Morgan get here?" Josh asked, as he drove the Bentley back to Bel Air. He was used to driving it now.

"She lands at eleven P.M. on Sunday. She should be at the house at midnight. She has a five P.M. flight back on Monday afternoon. She'll have to leave us by three to check in. She's going straight from the cemetery, after the service." He nodded, thinking again that she could at least have come for the weekend to offer some comfort, and spent Monday night with her mother to be with her at the reception and the night after the funeral. She might be an important surgeon, but no one was that important, and she did face-lifts for God's sake, Josh thought, not open-heart surgery. She seemed heartless to Josh, and totally self-centered, although he wouldn't have said that to Ardith, but he thought it at every limit and boundary Morgan set. Whatever her grievances about her childhood, which Ardith had alluded to and seemed to take full responsibility for, it seemed a poor excuse to Josh. His parents hadn't been supportive of his aspirations as an actor, but it never led him to take it out on them when they got older, became sick and frail, and finally died. He had respected who they were and what they meant to him, even if they didn't encourage his acting career, and they had had their own struggles in life, financially and in a difficult marriage. His father had been a drinker and had often been harsh with Josh as a boy, when he didn't measure up to his father's academic aspirations for him. He had been a hard taskmaster. His mother had been gentler. They had made sacrifices to send him to Juilliard, which Josh was grateful for, even though he had decided not to pursue music as his career. But the training and discipline had been excellent.

Morgan didn't seem to feel she owed her mother much of anything, and it saddened him for Ardith, who made few demands of her daughter. Morgan had made it clear that since her mother and Bill weren't married, she had no real obligation to be at his funeral, and a token appearance for part of it was good enough—which it wasn't, in Josh's opinion. What was happening now was about Ardith, not about her longtime companion. It was Ardith who needed the support that Morgan doled out so sparingly. It was as though she blamed her mother for her father's untimely death in disgrace years before, when in fact Ardith had been the victim of it, not the cause. It wasn't her fault that he was cheating on her and got exposed due to the fatal helicopter accident. Morgan's view of it was skewed, and she seemed to take it out on her mother at every opportunity, thirty-one years later, which was more than excessive. Events had punished Ardith at the time, and Morgan had been perpetuating it ever since. It was a long time to be punished, although Ardith seemed to have made her peace with it and was surprisingly forgiving of her daughter. It made Josh angry watching it. He was glad to be there to help Ardith.

As they drove toward Bel Air, he took a turnoff in Beverly Hills. Ardith was staring out the window, didn't notice, and didn't question it until they stopped at a small Italian restaurant, where he often ate when he could afford to go out to dinner.

"Where are we?" Ardith looked at him in surprise when he parked and turned off the car.

"Luigi's. They have the best pizza in L.A., and some really good pasta. You need to eat," he said quietly.

"I'm not hungry," she said matter-of-factly.

"I haven't seen you put food in your mouth since breakfast and that was half a piece of toast you didn't finish. The food is good here, and there are no paparazzi," he reassured her. "No one comes here." She was wearing jeans and a black sweater and big dark glasses, and he was sure no one would recognize her.

She laid her head back against the seat and smiled at him. "Thank you for taking such good care of me."

"As your official errand boy, that's my job." With everything that had happened, he was a lot more than that by then, and they both knew it. He had been more than a friend to her for the past two weeks, particularly in the week since Bill had died so unexpectedly. Josh had really stepped up to the plate even more than she knew, and she was grateful. "Come on, let's go eat. I'm starving." It hadn't occurred to her yet that the studio had ended his job and would no longer pay him. Her mind was so full of the funeral, and she was still so shocked, that it had obscured everything else.

"Me too," she admitted about being hungry, as they got out of the car. They could smell the pizza from the parking lot, and it smelled delicious.

"They have great spaghetti and meatballs too." Their dinner to-gether was spontaneous, but seeing Bill's casket had shaken her badly, and Josh wanted to do something to lift her spirits. She needed it desperately. She didn't want to see her friends, and Morgan was remaining aloof and distant and offering her mother no comfort, so he stepped in to provide what no one else did. He wanted to do it. Besides, she was barely eating and looked as though she had lost five or ten pounds that week. He was worried about her. The fact that she was a major star no longer mattered to either of them. She was just a woman who needed some compassion and kindness, and he was happy to supply it to a fellow human. He sensed that she would have done it for him.

She took off her dark glasses once they sat down in a back booth, and she ordered a simple pizza, and he ordered one with everything on it. The pizzas were as delicious as he had promised, and he talked her into sharing a hot fudge sundae with him after she finished her pizza. He was happy to see her eating enough for the first time in a week. She'd been living on snacks and PowerBars until then. She looked relaxed as she shared the sundae with him, and asked if they had sent him the promised script yet. All they had talked about all week was the funeral, but everything was organized by then.

"Of course not. I'll probably never hear about it again. No one in Hollywood likes to say no, so they just vanish and you never hear from them." She knew it was true.

"Until you finally get a break from someone. It'll come," she said confidently, and he smiled wryly at her.

"Thank you for your faith in me. You don't even know if I can act."

"Actually, I do," she said, smiling at him. "I had my agent get me copies of your last two horror movies and a particularly ghastly sci-fi movie. The scripts were awful, but you're a very credible actor, if they'd give you a decent script to work with. I have to admit, though, I did kind of love you as an alien." He laughed and was stunned. "I haven't been able to sleep, so they kept me entertained."

"You watched that crap? I'm mortified, but very touched."

"I wanted to see what kind of talent you have. You do have talent, you just need a good script to work with. I kind of liked you as the alien, except for the weird ears and the silver face." They both laughed and he couldn't believe she'd gone to the trouble of watching his movies. "I didn't like you as much as a vampire, and the girl you were biting kept squealing like a little pig instead of screaming." They were both in good spirits when they left the restaurant, and he was bowled over that Ardith Law had watched his horror movies and thought he had talent. It reminded him again that life was strange. Fate was more so, and you never knew what was going to happen.

They chatted all the way back to Bel Air. She felt human again, after a sundae and a pizza, and he felt like the luckiest man in the world to have her as a friend, even if he'd gotten there by being her errand boy.

When they got to the house, Oscar was waiting for Ardith at the front door, looked suspiciously at Josh, and started to growl at him. Josh picked him up in one hand, looked him in the eye, and said, "Oscar, knock it off," and then set him down gently on the floor. Oscar scampered off and was back a minute later carrying his favorite red ball and dropped it at Josh's feet as a peace offering. Josh threw it into the living room and Oscar went to fetch it and brought it back, wagging his tail. He had finally decided that Josh wasn't so bad after all. Ardith smiled at him.

"I think you have a new friend."

"It's about goddamn time," Josh said, throwing the red ball again. It had taken Oscar two weeks to decide that Josh was okay, and it had taken Ardith a lot less to figure that out. And as Josh gave Ardith a hug, and left a few minutes later, he knew that she was the most amazing woman he had ever met, and he had been blessed the day he met her. He had a friend.

While Ardith and Josh ate pizza and a hot fudge sundae at Luigi's, Morgan and Ben Ryan were having dinner at La Grenouille for their second date. He was a regular there and all the waiters and head-waiters knew him. He took women there often. The couple ordered foie gras as an appetizer, and they had lobster for dinner, and Ben had preordered chocolate soufflés for dessert. He had sent her long-stem roses earlier that week, in the palest ballet pink. He had sent them to her home so no one at the office would be aware of it. As promised, he was being discreet, although he reminded her that they were doing nothing wrong. It was no one's business that they were having dinner together. And he told her again at La Grenouille how special she was, and he had never felt this way before. He looked so sincere as he said it that she believed him. She fully believed that magic did happen, and one could meet one's soulmate later in life. After two dinners, she was beginning to believe that he was hers.

"Why don't you come to my apartment on Sunday? I'll cook for you," he suggested halfway through dinner, and she looked regretful as soon as he said it.

"I can't. I'd love to, but I have to go to L.A. to see my mother." She looked less than enthused at the prospect.

"Can you put it off a week or two? I love lazy Sundays. We can walk in the park, and watch movies, and then I'll make you dinner." It sounded heavenly to her, and a perfect setting for a romantic Sunday. All she could think of now was him, when she wasn't working and with patients. He filled her mind, and he looked just as besotted with her. Their budding romance had taken off at jet speed, and she wondered if that was how it happened with a man his age. He knew who and what he wanted, what suited him, and for now she was it. She felt the same way about him. He felt like The One to her, and she had never felt that way before.

"I wish I could put off the trip to L.A.," she said sincerely, "but I can't. I have to be at a funeral with her on Monday."

"That doesn't sound like fun," he said seriously.

"It won't be. I'm flying out Sunday, and I'll be back on Monday night."

"A family member or close friend?" Ben asked with a look of concern.

"Her partner and companion of twelve years. He died suddenly a week ago. He was seventy-eight years old but seemed in good health. He died in his sleep in London."

"How sad." But something about what Morgan said rang a bell for Ben, and he looked at her strangely. "This may sound crazy, but it wouldn't be William West, would it?" She nodded. She had told him very little about her family since they met, except that her father died when she was a child, and her mother was never around.

"Yes, it is sad," she said cautiously.

"Which means that your mother must be . . ." He looked stunned as it dawned on him. "Ardith Law?" She nodded again.

"Oh my God. That never occurred to me, but you look like her now that I know it. You didn't tell me."

"It sounds weird when you tell people your mother is a movie star." She smiled at him.

"She's more than that. She's an icon. She's an incredible actress. And you chose medicine instead?" He seemed surprised, although he realized now that her mother must be a lot to live up to, and Morgan had chosen not to try, which maybe was smart of her. And she had a great career of her own.

"I hated everything about Hollywood when I was growing up."

"And that would explain why she was never around. She's had an incredible career."

"Yes, she has, and she's very talented," Morgan conceded, looking childlike for a minute, "but she was always on location, making a movie somewhere else. I felt like an orphan. My father died when I was seven, so he was never around either. He was a producer-director, John Walker, and my mother's priority was always her career in those days. She's slowed down a little now, but only because good parts are harder to get at her age." Ben frowned for a minute and then looked at Morgan with a serious question.

"If I remember correctly, she's about my age. Does that feel strange to you to be going out with a man the same age as your parents, or is that something you've done before?" He wanted to know more about her, and Morgan doled out information sparingly.

"No, I never have dated anyone my mother's age," she said easily, "but to be honest, I'm loving it. It's wonderful to be out with an adult. You make dates and keep them, you don't seem to play games, you're not dating four women at the same time. You seem to know what you want and go straight for it. Men my age have always been disappointing and play so many games. I'd rather be out with someone who has gotten past all that and knows what they want."

"You have a good point. Men grow up a lot slower than women. But younger women can be complicated too, and from about thirty on, they're obsessed with marriage and babies. I don't want to deal with all that. I'm delighted to see that it doesn't seem to be an issue with you."

"I've never been obsessed with getting married," Morgan said honestly, "and I'm pretty sure I don't want kids. I didn't enjoy being one, and I don't think I'd like having one." He smiled at what she said. "I just want a straightforward relationship with a man I love and who loves me, on an equal basis, as two mature adults. And if not, then I'd rather be alone. I've never chased after a relationship. I figured that the right one would find me, and in the meantime, I'm busy and I love my work."

Ben reached across the table and took her hand in his and held it. "It sounds like a perfect match to me," he whispered to her. "I knew it the first time I saw you when I walked into your office. I felt like I was going to explode. Morgan, you're the sexiest woman I've ever seen, if it isn't rude to say that on a second date." She was immensely flattered. She knew that many of the men she had dated found her cold, and sometimes she had been. Ben was the first man who had gotten over her walls that quickly and stolen her heart.

"I feel the same way," she whispered shyly. She loved his mind, and everything he said, how he treated her, the level of elegance and sophistication around him, and he was the best-looking man she had ever seen. He was drop-dead handsome, and she felt her heart pound every time she looked at him. He could read easily in the adoring look in her eyes how she felt about him. When she wasn't with him, she fantasized about him constantly. She had been desperate to see him that night, which was why she hadn't gone to L.A. sooner to be with her mother that weekend. She wanted to be with Ben if she could, and once he invited her out for Friday night, wild horses couldn't have dragged her to L.A. a minute before Sunday, despite her mother's grief. Bill wasn't her father after all, she didn't owe him anything, and Morgan thought her mother was strong enough to deal with the loss on her own. Being with her for the funeral on Monday seemed like enough. It was what she had told herself to justify staying in New York for the weekend and seeing Ben.

"You probably think I've said the same things to a million women, but I haven't. There have been a lot of women in my life, but never the right ones. I've married twice and made a grave mistake both times. I think I've been looking for you all my life. I knew it the first time I saw you. I think you're the one I've been waiting for, and now that I've found you, I don't intend to let you go. I think that's why this has taken off so quickly. I don't want to waste another minute. I'm sixty-three years old, and I want to grab what we've got and hold on to it. I'm in love with you, Morgan. I never believed in love at first sight before. Now I do."

"It's lucky you weren't involved with anyone else when we met," she said quietly.

"I won't pretend to you that I've been living like a monk." She knew he had a reputation as a womanizer, which wasn't surprising given his celebrity and successful career on TV for the past thirty years. "And there may be a few glum faces around town for a day or two when people find out about us, but I've never made promises I didn't intend to deliver on. I've dated a lot of women, but I've never felt about anyone the way I do about you or said the things I am saying to you. I think we were made for each other. I'm just sorry it took me so long to find you," he said, beaming at her.

Morgan drank a fair amount of excellent champagne at dinner, which didn't matter since she wasn't on call the next day and she could relax. She never drank the night before she went on duty or if she was on call, and they'd had a bottle of Château Margaux bordeaux at dinner too. Neither of them was drunk, but they'd had a good amount of wine, left the restaurant after dinner arm-in-arm, and as soon as they were outside, he put his arms around her and kissed her passionately. After everything he had said to her at dinner, her response was immediate and equally passionate as she melted into his arms.

"Will you come home with me?" he whispered to her. She smiled and nodded and he kissed her again. She got into the car he had waiting for them, and his driver took them to his apartment on Central Park West. It was a beautiful duplex, with a spectacular view of the park, which was still dusted with white from a recent snowfall, and he led her to his bedroom, where he gently laid her on the bed and made love to her until they fell asleep when the sun came up. She had never had a night like it in her life. Some of the men her own age she had slept with had been proficient lovers, although they were more athletic than romantic, but no one had ever taken her to the heights Ben did, or said the same things to her. She felt as though she had died and gone to heaven when she fell asleep and awoke the next morning in his arms. It felt more like a honeymoon than a first time. They showered together and he gave her one of his bathrobes to wear. He cooked breakfast for her in his kitchen looking out over the park, and then they went back to bed and made love again.

She stayed with him until Sunday morning, after another magical night of passion, and then she went home to her apartment to pack hastily for Bill's funeral. She hated to leave Ben, but it would only be for twenty-four hours, or two days at most. She was glad she hadn't agreed to spend the weekend in L.A. She would have missed the most incredible weekend of her life with Ben, and the best sex she'd ever had.

"When can I see you again?" he asked her when she was leaving.

"I'll be back Monday night, and I have back-to-back surgeries on Tuesday, but I'm free Tuesday night."

"You'll be exhausted," he said sympathetically. "Let's make it Wednesday. Why don't you stay here again?" he suggested, and she nodded. "We can do something fun on the weekend. I have to go to China the following week, to do a story there, and I'm stopping in London on the way home. I'll only be gone a week. I travel a lot," he warned her, but it didn't surprise her in his job. He was introducing her to his life now. Hers was entirely based in New York, but he traveled all over the world, which was exciting. Everything about him was dazzling compared to the men she'd known. She was in a whole other universe now, out in the stratosphere with him, and she was loving every minute of it. It was heady stuff, almost like a drug. But he already seemed just as addicted to her. She'd never experienced anything like it and knew she never would again. And she had no intention of telling her mother, who would probably say something negative about it, warn her to be careful, and disapprove of his age. But Morgan could sense that Ben was for real. She wasn't worried and was reaching for the prize with both hands.

He kissed her all the way out the door and texted her when she got home. He said that every moment away from her was unbearable and he couldn't wait till Wednesday when she saw him again. It was only three days away but felt like an eternity to both of them.

She felt like she was floating when she went through security at the airport and boarded the plane to L.A., and just before the plane took off, he texted her. "I will love you forever," he said with a giant red heart. She just had enough time to text him a red heart in response, and turned off her phone. She had no idea how the miracle of Ben Ryan had come into her life, but she wanted to hold on to him. She had never been as taken with any man in her life. And the fact that he was twenty-five years older didn't bother her at all. If anything, it made him seem sexier and more mature. She already knew without any doubt that he was The One for her.

Chapter 6

On Sunday night, Josh and Ardith went over all the details together for the funeral the next day. The seating, the ushers, the pallbearers, the security, the flowers, the music. The programs had been delivered that afternoon and were beautiful. Two directors and a producer were going to read eulogies. The police were putting up cordons outside the church to keep the fans at a distance. The viewing at the funeral home had gone smoothly, with adequate security, but had taken hours. Josh had spent part of the afternoon there to make sure that things went well. There was a mountain of flowers people had brought to leave for Bill as they walked by.

Josh and Ardith ate pizza while they went over their notes in her kitchen. He had been vitally efficient helping her organize the funeral. She wanted it to be perfect for Bill, and Josh was seeing to it that it would be. It was a labor of love he was doing for her, and she was deeply grateful. They had been working together for hours, and had seen to everything, when he got up to leave.

"Try to get some sleep tonight. You're going to need it tomorrow," he said gently. He had changed out of his black suit after the viewing and was wearing a faded band T-shirt, torn jeans, and biker boots, and had come on his Harley, which Ardith didn't object to now. She was grateful for his help with all the funeral details, and he was just saying good night when they heard the front door open. A minute later Morgan walked into the kitchen and was surprised to see Josh standing there with her mother. She didn't know who he was at first, and Ardith introduced them. Morgan looked at him coldly and said a terse hello. She was tired from the trip, and he looked a mess after hours of work with Ardith on the funeral. She hadn't expected to find a stranger with her mother.

Josh's reaction to her wasn't warm either. He watched her greet her mother coolly and hug her, and he thought she should have gotten there days before instead of at the eleventh hour.

"How was the flight?" Ardith asked her.

"Long." She had talked to Ben on the way into the city, and she missed him, but didn't mention him to her mother. Josh noticed the resemblance between mother and daughter, but Morgan was the ice-cold version, a frigid beauty, in contrast to her much more human, warmer, and actually more beautiful mother.

"Do you want something to eat?" Ardith asked her daughter, as Josh picked up a stack of papers to take with him. It was the seating for the service, which he wanted to put into better order for the ushers. Some of the ushers and all the pallbearers were famous actors who had been Bill's friends and wanted to help at the service.

"I ate on the plane, it was disgusting, as usual," Morgan said, casting glances at Josh, hoping to make him feel unwelcome. She wanted to be alone with her mother. A few minutes later he left, and Morgan turned to her. "What's he doing here at this hour?"

"We had a lot of details to go over for tomorrow."

"How much longer is he going to be working for you?"

"He has six more weeks in his contract, and he's been incredibly helpful. I couldn't have put it all together without him."

"He's taking advantage of you, Mom. You should let him go after the funeral."

"Why? Are you coming out here to help me get Bill's things in order? That would certainly be useful," Ardith said ironically, slightly annoyed at Morgan, who seemed to be resentful of any assistance her mother had, while offering none herself.

"I don't have time, and you know it," Morgan said tersely, and Ardith nodded.

"Then you should be grateful someone else does and is willing to help me," she said clearly, and Morgan went to drop off her bag in the guest room where she stayed in her mother's house. Her original bedroom had been turned into a study for Bill when he moved in ten years before, which still annoyed her, although she hardly ever came to L.A. anymore, and used every excuse not to. Morgan was back in the kitchen a few minutes later and made herself a cup of tea.

"Is it going to be a circus tomorrow?" she said with a disapproving look.

"It's going to be a final farewell to a major Hollywood figure, and a service worthy of him," Ardith said quietly. "What are you so angry about?" Morgan wasn't even sure herself, but she always was when she saw her mother. She had begrudged all the attention Ardith lavished on Bill, when Morgan had been deprived of it herself during her childhood. And now there was some young guy ingratiating himself to her mother, dressed like a homeless person, in Morgan's opinion, whom her mother was clearly grateful to. Someone else was always getting Ardith's attention and affection, and Morgan resented them for it, and for the help they gave her mother, which she had never wanted to give. She felt as though she had been replaced by others for years now. But they were kind to Ardith, and she wasn't. It was a vicious circle. She and Ardith never did well at close range. Morgan's longstanding resentment of her mother came through her pores and she couldn't control it.

"I don't know why you wanted me to come out," Morgan grumbled, sipping her tea in the kitchen. "You have more than enough people to take care of you, and I had patients to see in New York," she said, sounding important, which she was in her own world.

"I only have one daughter and I may not have been married to Bill, but he meant a great deal to me, and it's a loss. It means a lot to me that you came, even just for the funeral."

"I can only stay for the service and the burial. You'll have to use the rest of your support team for the reception. I don't know why you're giving a reception. This isn't a wedding."

"No, it isn't, but this is what people do at funerals. They celebrate the life of the person who died, they share memories, they cry with each other. It's comforting."

"It sounds morbid to me."

"Well, you won't be here, so you don't need to worry about it." Ardith hated her daughter's rigidity and her coldness, her lack of compassion for others and especially for her mother. Ardith always believed that it was because Morgan was an unhappy person. She had never had a man in her life she really loved, didn't want a husband and children. She loved her job, but she was determined to carry the bitter torch of her childhood forever and fuel her anger at her mother. Nothing ever seemed to make it better. "It was nice of you to come out," Ardith repeated. "Bill would have appreciated it."

"I'm sure he wouldn't have cared," Morgan countered. "We probably didn't speak more than a dozen times in all the years I knew him. We had nothing to say to each other, except about his latest movie. That's all he ever talked about."

"He had a very narrow focus on life, but he was a good person." He wasn't fascinating or brilliant, but he was kind and he had been good to Ardith, and she wanted to pay homage to that now. Morgan didn't care and wanted to be sure her mother knew it. She had an incredible ability to hurt people with her cold manner and sharp tongue, which had gotten sharper with age. She hadn't mellowed, and Ardith was sorry to see it. At some point, the anger ceased to wound, and just became tiresome for others to listen to, even though it was intended to injure. It had stopped hurting Ardith as much as it used to, a long time since. Therapy had helped her to endure it, and a certain amount of faith had helped her to forgive it, but it made their encounters difficult and painful, and Ardith always wondered how Morgan managed to keep the fires of her anger stoked after this many years. Apparently, hell had no fury like a daughter who felt she had been slighted and deprived in her youth. She doubted Morgan would ever get over it. She had never forgiven her mother. And nothing in her life had softened the sharp edges of her bitterness over her neglected childhood. She wore it like a mantle of porcupine quills, which made it hard to be around her. And Ardith was suddenly glad she hadn't come any sooner.

She was surprised when Josh called her that night as she was getting into bed. Morgan had retired half an hour earlier, as soon as she finished her tea.

"Are you okay?" he asked her cautiously. He didn't want to intrude on her family, what there was of it. But he hated the way Morgan spoke to her mother and was shocked by it.

"I'm fine," Ardith reassured him.

"Morgan seemed so angry. I was afraid she might get into an argument with you."

"I know better. She's always like that. She has been for years."

"She's so different from you." There was none of Ardith's gentle wisdom, her caring for others, her compassion, or her humor. "She's a very angry woman."

"I hear she's nicer to her patients," Ardith said fairly.

"That doesn't do much for you. Will you be okay tomorrow?" Josh was genuinely concerned about Ardith.

"I'll have to be. And she won't stay long. She's leaving from the burial. She's not coming to the reception."

"I'll do whatever I can for you. Just give me a wave, and I'll be there." He was planning to watch it all from a slight distance, so he had an overview and could see any problems as they happened.

"You're the best errand boy in the world," she said, and he laughed.

"At your service anytime, Ms. Law." She was touched that he had called her before he went to bed. Morgan would have had a fit if she knew. It was almost as though she was jealous of everyone, which seemed ridiculous to Ardith. Ardith had a right to whatever help she needed. And Josh had been incredibly kind and beyond helpful ever since Bill died and she had to organize the funeral.

She was up early the next day, and in the kitchen when Morgan came to make a cup of tea and eat some cereal. Ardith was making some final notes about the seating, and went to get dressed shortly after. She reappeared in a chic black Chanel suit with a black satin collar, black stockings, high-heeled black suede pumps, and a very elegant black hat she'd had for several years and never worn, which was perfect for the occasion. Morgan was wearing a simple black dress and coat, and her bag was packed to put in the car and take to the funeral so she could go directly to the airport.

Josh arrived in a black suit, with a white shirt and black tie, and sat in the front seat of the Rolls on the way to the funeral. Ardith had a driver she used for special occasions. Josh didn't say anything to Ardith in the car, because he didn't want to annoy Morgan and have her take it out on her mother. She appeared to be on the verge of fury at all times, and he was sorry Ardith had to put up with her, especially at such a hard time, at the funeral of her longtime partner.

The funeral was as beautiful as Ardith had wanted it to be, and Bill would have loved it. Hundreds of people filled the church. The eulogies were touching, and even funny. The flowers were exquisite, and the burial was short and painfully sweet. Paparazzi ringed the proceedings at all times, with long lenses, and took photographs of all the stars who were there, and particularly Ardith, who looked spectacular in the hat with just a wisp of a veil over her eyes. She looked years younger than she was, and heartbreakingly beautiful. And watching her, Josh began to understand why Morgan was so angry. Her mother was a star to her very core, without trying to be, without showing off, without lifting a finger, and Morgan had none of her charm or warmth or ease with people. She was burning with jealousy of her mother. With all her accomplishments and her own talents, she had never found her own center, and she hated her mother for everything she herself wasn't. She had no distinct identity of her own that Josh could see, and he suspected that she had never loved another human being. Ardith was a woman who had loved and lost, tried and been hurt, and had given Bill West years of comfort, even if she had no passion for him.

She loved her daughter in ways Morgan couldn't understand and didn't have within her, with compassion and forgiveness. Ardith was fire and Morgan was ice, and every contact with her mother scalded her and made her feel inadequate again. Josh guessed that Morgan had never found herself and blamed her mother for it. And all she could think of to pin it on were her mother's absences while making movies when Morgan was a child. Morgan's anger had become her identity, and she couldn't give it up or there would be nothing left of her at all. She was a ghost, with no form, no heart, and no soul, a phantom of what she might have been if she had learned to love and give of herself, but she was too afraid to do it. She wanted to love and be loved but she had no idea how. Josh felt sorry for her as he watched her. And when she left her mother at the cemetery, her arms were stiff as Ardith hugged her. Ardith held her for a moment and kissed her, and thanked her for coming, and then Morgan hurried to the car and driver waiting for her and never looked back as she drove away, as Ardith stood and watched her. Then Ardith went back to the grave to say a last goodbye to the man she knew she hadn't loved enough, but who had been satisfied with what she gave him, which was some small consolation now. He had made being with him so easy for her, and so comfortable. She left a single white rose next to the grave, and then walked to the car where Josh was waiting for her with the driver. She had greeted hundreds of people at the church and the cemetery, and now she had the reception to get through. It was an exhausting day for her. Josh looked at her carefully as she got into the car.

"How are you holding up?" he whispered to her.

"I'm okay," she said with a small smile. "The seating worked out perfectly. I was afraid we'd forgotten someone and it would be like playing musical chairs." He smiled and they drove away. Josh was impressed that she hadn't forgotten a single detail or a single person. Every major star in Hollywood had had a seat and was accounted for. The reception at the Bel-Air was going to be free-form, with people eating, drinking, and remembering, in a large handsome room and as they strolled in the gardens and admired the swans.

Josh followed her into the melee when they got out at the hotel. Three hundred people had been invited, and the paparazzi were lying in wait for Ardith when she left the car. He wanted to protect her from the cameras and prying eyes, but he knew there was no way he could, so he just followed her to the reception, stayed on the fringes watching her, and brought her something to drink when she seemed like she needed it. She finally left the reception at six o'clock, and looked drained when they got to the house. It was then that Morgan would have been of some comfort to her, but she was long gone, and in the air on the way to New York. The house was silent and empty. Bill was gone. Morgan had left. Benicia had gone to the funeral and had gone home. Josh was the only one in the house with Ardith. It touched him that she was so alone in her life.

"Go to bed," Josh said gently to her. "You've had a hell of a day."

"I know, but it was beautiful, wasn't it?" she said, as she tossed her hat on a chair.

"He would have loved it. It was a noble send-off," Josh said, and she smiled. "You need to go to bed now." Josh had already agreed to pack up Bill's things with her that week, but he was worried about her now. She looked pushed to her limits and worn out.

She disappeared for a few minutes and came back in a nightgown and comfortable old bathrobe. All the trappings of stardom were gone, the Chanel suit, the elegant hat, the high heels. She was just a woman like any other, and sat down in the kitchen with him, grateful to have him there. He had taken off his suit jacket and his tie.

"I think every major star in Hollywood was there," she said. "They were all afraid to miss it." He laughed. "I'm glad Morgan didn't stay," she added honestly, and he nodded. "Her anger exhausts me. You've seen how she is now. I don't know how she keeps her rage going after all these years."

"She's jealous of you," he said simply, afraid to overstep a line.

"I suppose she is. It's silly of her. I could never have gotten through medical school or do what she does."

"But she's not you. She's not a star," he said quietly.

"She never wanted to be."

"Yes, she did, she just didn't know it, or have the guts to try, so she hates you for who you are." Ardith shook her head in dismay, but knew he was right.

"I hope she finds what she wants someday," Ardith said. "She'll be miserable until she does. I always thought the right man would make her happy, but she hasn't found him yet."

"He'd have to have a thick skin to love her," Josh said. Ardith nodded and looked at Josh seriously again.

"Thank you for being there today. I've known some of those people for most of my life, but none of them would have done all that you did." She had felt genuinely supported and protected by him, in the kindest way.

"If I leave, will you go to bed?" he asked, concerned.

"I might." She smiled at him. "See you tomorrow? Or are you too tired to come to work?"

"I wouldn't miss it," he said, picking up his jacket and tie off the chair. "See you in the morning. And Ardith, you did a great job." It was who she was, he knew now. The consummate perfectionist, down to the last detail. The hardest worker he had ever known, and a real person to the tips of her fingers, and not a diva at all. She was the strongest woman he had ever met, and yet vulnerable at the same time. He wanted to do whatever he could for her, to protect her and give back some of what she gave. He wasn't sure how to do that, but he wanted to. And he only had six weeks left to spend with her.

The thought of leaving her pained him. He worried about what would happen to her when he left. He even wanted to protect her from her daughter.

He closed the door softly behind him. Oscar barked once when he left, and then followed Ardith to her bedroom, where she lay down on her bed and closed her eyes for a minute and fell into a deep sleep and didn't wake until morning.

She felt as though she had been beaten when she got up the next day, but she was up and dressed, in jeans and a sweatshirt, when Josh came to work.

He looked like he'd been on a two-week drunk. He hadn't shaved or combed his hair and she laughed when she saw him. "You look like I feel, like I got dragged behind a horse on a rope yesterday."

"That sounds about right." He smiled at her, and groaned when he sat down. She put a cup of coffee down in front of him and he drank it gratefully. "What are we doing today?" he asked her after a second cup.

"I know it's soon, but I don't want to be looking at Bill's things all over the house, it's too sad. You talked to the museum. I want to box everything up and send it to them this week. We're on a roll after the funeral. I'm afraid that if I stop now, I'll fall apart. There's a lot to do." She wanted to pack everything up so she didn't have to look at it and drown in memories. She didn't want lingering reminders of the past. She had done the same when John Walker died, and gotten rid of everything quickly. It had helped her then, and she thought it would now. She didn't want to cling to sadness. She wanted to remember Bill's life.

Josh followed her to Bill's dressing room where they packed all his clothes in neat boxes, and a few boxes of mementos she wanted to keep. She put photographs in another box, and Benicia came to help throw things away. By that afternoon, Bill's dressing room was empty. They still had his study to do, with all his books and papers and the souvenirs of a fifty-year career. The Hollywood Museum had the most extensive collection of Hollywood memorabilia in the world. Costumes, props, photographs, scripts, personal papers, cars, posters. They were thrilled to be receiving the entire personal collection of William West.

In the end, it took three days to pack everything, with a little help from Benicia, but mostly Josh and Ardith did it. She was going to use his study herself. It was a small sunny room, and she had enough clothes to fill his closets. Josh helped her with all of it, and when they finished, they put all the boxes in the garage. She was using a moving service to take them to the museum, and she had no regrets about what she was giving up. She had kept the photographs she loved, of Bill at his best.

When they'd put the last box in the garage, Josh looked at her and told her to get a jacket.

"Where are we going?"

"You'll see. We need to get out of here." Ardith didn't argue with him, she wanted to get out of the house too. She felt as though she had swum through a tidal wave of Bill's belongings and memories for the past three days, and had cried several times. She had no idea he had collected so much stuff and stashed it in every nook and cranny. It was gone now, which was a relief. She had her memories of their years together, which was enough. She didn't want mourning him to become her new job, or the essence of her existence. She needed to go on living and make a life for herself without him.

Josh was waiting for her outside, and handed her a helmet when she walked out the kitchen door.

"What's that for?"

"Put it on."

"Oh God, you're going to risk my life on that thing." She looked suspiciously at his Harley parked near her back door.

"I'm not going to risk your life. I promise I'll go slow. We're just going to take a little ride," he said, smiling at her. "Hold on to me. We're not going far."

"I rode on the back of a Vespa in Rome once, when I was about twenty-four. I never thought I'd survive it."

"You were lucky you did. I'm not Italian, this isn't Rome, and this is no Vespa. It's as solid as a rock," he said, as she swung her leg over the seat and snuggled up behind him with the helmet on and her arms around his waist.

"If the paparazzi catch us doing this, I'll be front page on every tabloid," she warned him. As she said it, he handed her a pair of goggles and she put them on.

"No one will recognize you," he promised, hoping he was right. They headed down her driveway and onto the street a minute later, and he reached a gentle speed as she laughed. It was an amazing feeling of freedom as she rode behind him, and he was right, she needed to get out of the house and away from the boxes of Bill's things. She needed to feel wind on her face, and fresh air in her lungs. She wondered where they were going and then saw that he was taking her to the beach. The ocean was calm and flat and the sky was blue. He parked the Harley, and they took off their shoes and walked onto the sand. He smiled at her, and grabbed her hand, and they ran down to the water and let it wash over their feet as they walked along the wet sand. It was the perfect counterpoint to what they'd been doing for three days, their preparations for the funeral, and all the mournful duties they had carried out since Bill died. They ran along next to each other until they couldn't run anymore. Josh picked up a few small rocks and skipped them over the water, and they watched the waves come in, and then they walked up to the dry sand and sat down. It was exactly what Ardith needed. She leaned her head onto his shoulder as she sat next to him, and he smiled down at her.

"Thank you," she said gratefully, as they watched the surf, and the sun setting slowly. "I feel alive again. I was beginning to feel dead myself. Dealing with death is so exhausting."

"You need to have some fun now. It's been a heavy two weeks." When he said it, it reminded her that he'd be leaving her in a few weeks. His job with her would be over. It already was now, but he had stayed on to help her after Bill died. She still had no idea that he was no longer being paid for it, and thought he was completing the job.

"What am I going to do without you when you leave?" She had gotten so used to having Josh around every day that not seeing him every morning seemed sad to her now. She had to remind herself at times that he was getting paid to be there with her, that this wasn't some kind of date, or a favor he was doing her, it was a job, or at least she thought it was.

"I'm going to miss you too," he said softly, as the sun went down and there was a sudden chill in the air. "I keep thinking about it. I don't want this to end." She didn't know how to respond.

"I'd hire you, but it would be selfish of me. You need to go back to acting instead of babysitting for aging divas."

"You're not aging or a diva. You're younger than anyone I know, and you're not much of a diva."

"I'm not much of a star either. I haven't made a picture in two years."

"You will one of these days, when the right script comes along."

"So will you," Ardith said firmly, and Josh turned to look at her and saw all the honesty in her eyes that always touched his heart. She was so wide open and true to herself, and so honest with the world, he knew now what a rare person she was, and he could no longer run from what he felt for her, or hide it from her. Without saying a word he pulled her into his arms and kissed her. She was shocked at first, and then gave in to it and kissed him back. They sat there for a long time, and then she looked at him and shook her head.

"You can't do that," she said softly.

"Why not?" He was afraid he had made a terrible mistake and ruined everything.

"Because I'm twenty-one years older than you are, and you deserve better than this, not some old woman who'll hold you back. You need a girl half my age who'll marry you and give you babies and the life you deserve. Don't settle for someone like me, Josh," she said seriously.

"This isn't settling, this is my wildest dream come true. There's no one else in this world like you. I'd be the luckiest man alive to be with you."

"I'm old. I'll be sick and bedridden one day, and you'd be a nurse. I don't want that for you. I had it with Bill—he was deteriorating slowly, I know what it's like. And he was only sixteen years older, I'm five years more than that."

"You're still young. We could have great years ahead. I don't want some twenty-five-year-old girl, or kids. I've never wanted kids. I'm a kid myself. I want to be a kid with you," he said, and she laughed and gave him a shove.

"Maybe I should adopt you. I kept trying to think of ways to keep you with me. This wasn't what I had in mind," she said, "and anything I could think of would be unfair to you. You deserve so much more than what I am now. I'm sixty-two years old. You could be my son."

"But I'm not. Then marry me. That would be a full-time job."

"You're insane. I won't do that to you," she insisted, and he kissed her again, and she couldn't resist him.

"I don't care what you say. I'm not leaving you. I'd be lost without you now. You cleaned up my act and made me grow up in the last few weeks."

"Terrific. I'm proud of you. Now go find a girl your own age."

"I don't want a girl my age. They're a pain in the ass. Look at Morgan. She would drive me insane in a day."

"That's different. She's angry. Not all women her age are like her. Besides, she would go nuts if she thought we were together like that."

"I think she suspected I have feelings for you when she was here. Would you care what she thought about us?"

Ardith thought about it for a moment and shook her head. "No." As hard as Morgan had been on her for years, she didn't owe her that.

"Good. Then there's no one to object," he said smugly.

"*I* object. You deserve better than someone my age."

"I don't give a damn about your age. I love *you,* whatever age you are."

"I'm sixty-two, in case you've forgotten," she reminded him.

"I don't give a damn. I'm not impressed."

"Well, you should be."

"I'm the luckiest man alive to be even this close to you," he said with such feeling that she looked at him, shocked by everything he'd said.

"Are you serious?" Part of her hoped he wasn't, and another part wished he was, as crazy as that seemed.

"Completely," he said, without hesitating.

"You've lost your mind." It had gotten cold by then and she was shivering. He pulled her up from the sand and raced her back to where they had left the Harley. They were panting and out of breath when they got there. They had walked a long way down the beach.

"This is completely upside down," she said to him. "You can't fall in love with someone my age."

"Too late. I already did." He kissed her lightly on the lips and handed her the helmet and goggles as she stared at him.

"Josh, you can't do this. I won't let you."

"It's not up to you. It happens. You can't control everything in the world," he said. He kissed her again, and she didn't argue this time. It was an impossible situation, and she was determined not to get pulled into the fantasy with him, but he was hard to resist. He got on the bike then, and she got on behind him and put her arms around him, thinking of everything he had said.

They stopped for burgers at a remote ramshackle restaurant he knew on the way home, and she looked around and laughed.

"You take me to the worst places," she scolded him, but the burgers were good, and they shared a milkshake.

"Who else would take you to a place like this?"

"No one I know," she said.

"Exactly. How could you miss out on a life like this?"

"Think of your career. You need to look sexy to your fans. No one will hire you if you're with someone my age."

"That's not true. And who cares? This is our life, not theirs. And I'm in love with you. I can't help who I fall in love with. You put a spell on me, so now you have to deal with it." He took her home by the back roads so he didn't scare her on the Harley. They walked in through the back door and stood in her kitchen, and he looked at her for a long time and then gently reached out to her and pulled her close, and all his passion for her rose up in him like a wave he couldn't stop, and all the years that she had been celibate because of Bill's prostate surgery caught up with her, and before they could stop, they were in her bedroom, on her bed, making love like two starving people who had seen food for the first time and could no longer hold back. Everything they hadn't let themselves feel for each other took over, and it felt like fireworks lighting up the sky when they came.

They lay breathless in each other's arms afterward and he smiled at her. "I love you, Ardith Law, no matter what anyone says or thinks or does, and no matter what you say. I love you more than I've ever loved anyone in this world."

"I love you too," she said softly, knowing that what they were doing was crazy and maybe all wrong, but it was the happiest she had been in years.

Chapter 7

Ardith shook Josh gently awake just before eight o'clock the next morning, as Oscar yawned and stretched between them. He gave Josh a look as though to remind him he didn't belong there, and Josh smiled as soon as he opened an eye and saw Ardith, naked next to him in bed.

"I didn't realize this was going to be a threesome," he said, petting the poodle, who got up and licked his face.

"We have to get up," Ardith said in an urgent whisper.

"Why?" he asked her with a meaningful look. He had other plans with fresh morning energy he wanted to spend on her. He gently reached out and touched her breast, and she responded instantly.

"Benicia will be here any minute. We have to get up and look respectable."

"Oh. For Benicia?" Josh was disappointed and surprised.

"Bill's been gone for barely three weeks, and now I'm in bed with you. She'll think I'm a slut." He looked pensive for a minute and reluctantly agreed with her. Ardith had examined her own conscience the night before and realized that she had been faithful to Bill for twelve years, even once he could no longer make love to her. She didn't feel guilty now about her feelings for Josh, or her actions. They were honest and heartfelt, and Bill had had his due during his lifetime. His time had come and gone, and she was still here. But she realized that others might not see it as she did. And things were happening quickly with Josh.

"Do you want me to leave and come back?" he asked her, as Oscar lay on his back between them and went back to sleep. He seemed to have no objection to the new arrangement, as long as he could continue to sleep in her bed.

"No, let's just get dressed and make it look like you came to work early. Besides, if you leave on the Harley, the whole neighborhood will hear you. I'm supposed to look like the grieving widow."

"You weren't married to him," he reminded her.

"That's a detail. People forget things like that."

"Do you feel guilty?" he asked her, worried.

"No, I don't." She hadn't told him before, but thought she should now. "We hadn't had sex in over five years. He had prostate surgery, which made it impossible. And I stayed faithful to him."

"You're a saint," Josh said with a look of amazement, as he got out of bed in his full naked glory and she admired the beauty of his perfectly toned body. Hers was nowhere near as remarkable, although she was still beautiful, and in great shape for her age. She got up and put on a robe. She would have liked to make love to him again before they got up, but she wanted to be in the kitchen with him when

Benicia came to work, for now at least. They could break Benicia in to the new regime gradually. Ardith didn't want to shock her. She'd been fond of Bill, and was a deeply religious woman.

Josh came back from the bathroom a minute later, put on his underwear he retrieved from the floor, and his jeans. He pulled his T-shirt on, while Ardith got her own clothes on hastily and then she looked at him and laughed.

"I think your shirt is on inside out, or backwards or something." He checked and it was both. He fixed it and then hunted for his socks but couldn't find them.

"Did you put my socks somewhere?"

"No. Don't worry about it, she's not going to check if you're wearing socks, as long as you have your pants on." Ardith was wearing jeans and a sweatshirt. She and Josh didn't look fresh or well dressed, but they looked respectable enough. She made coffee for both of them, and they were at the kitchen table, looking casual, when Benicia unlocked the back door three minutes later. Ardith was reading the newspaper, and Josh was making notes and handing them to Ardith as though it was a work project. All the notes said "I love you." And Benicia marched off to the laundry room to start her day.

"Do you think we passed?" Josh whispered to Ardith, and she laughed.

"With flying colors."

"None of the women I've gone out with live with their parents, so I haven't dealt with this walk of shame shit since college. We'll have to break the news to her eventually. I wanted to make love to you when I woke up."

"Me too," she whispered back. Benicia had put a cramp in their style that morning. "We'll make up for it later."

After breakfast, Ardith went to put some of her papers in the desk Bill had used in her now-reclaimed study, and she found more of Bill's notes and files. She boxed them up for the museum. Josh took the box out to the garage, and reorganized some of the tools in a utility closet. Before lunch, he went home to shower and change his clothes, and right before he left Benicia walked into the kitchen with a puzzled expression, holding up two black socks.

"I found these under your pillow," she said to Ardith, as Josh struggled to keep a straight face.

"Oscar must have put them there. They're Bill's, they must have fallen out of one of the boxes." They were sending Bill's elegant wardrobe to the museum, and small basic items like underwear and socks were going to Goodwill. But the socks Benicia held up were Josh's and Oscar must have taken them and hid them.

"I thought so," Benicia said. "Poor Oscar, he must miss Mr. Bill." Oscar seemed perfectly content with the new arrangement, which Ardith couldn't say to her faithful housekeeper, at least not this soon.

"Lucky it wasn't my underwear," Josh whispered to her when Benicia left the room, and then left to go to his apartment. He was going to bring back some clothes so he could change in the morning, so he would look properly dressed when Benicia arrived. It had been a close call that morning. But it was all new to them, and a nice problem to have. Things were looking up.

Ardith spent the day feeling distracted and remorseful, not because of Bill, but because she thought that Josh was making a terrible mistake. He was infatuated with her, she told herself, and he needed to be with a much younger woman, not someone her age, who would rob him of his youth and the fun he could have with a girl even younger than he was. She was too old for him, and she intended to tell him that again after Benicia left that afternoon.

When he got back in a fresh collared shirt and clean jeans, he handed her a thick envelope.

"Look what came." He beamed at her.

"What is it?"

"It's the script they said they'd send me." He looked pleased and excited.

"Can I read it?" she asked him.

"Of course. I want to know what you think of it. We can share it." He trusted her advice implicitly. What better mentor could he have than a two-time Oscar winner?

"We'll read it tonight," she promised. She couldn't wait to see it and find out if the part they were offering was worth his time, or just another junk movie. She still wanted to introduce Josh to her agent. She had mentioned him to Joe Ricci, and on her recommendation, her agent said he was happy to meet him. He usually represented more established actors, who had several big movies behind them, but he was willing to consider Josh if Ardith said he was good and had talent.

They puttered around the house that day, passing time. After packing up all of Bill's possessions, and with the funeral over, they had no big projects at the moment. Josh took Oscar for a walk, and Ardith answered a stack of condolence letters, and finally, after leaving Ardith some food in the refrigerator, Benicia left. Josh gave a whoop of glee when she did and raced into Ardith's bedroom looking for her. He found her in her study, and she looked up with a grin when she saw him.

"Is she gone?" she asked him, standing up and walking toward him. They had both been waiting for the housekeeper to leave, so they could pursue what they had wanted to do that morning, and couldn't because she was due to arrive any minute.

Josh followed Ardith to her bedroom, unbuttoned her shirt and jeans, and slipped his hand inside them as she moaned. She pulled his shirt off and pulled down his jeans and released him in all his splendor. Their clothes were in a heap on the floor in minutes and they were on her bed, discovering the wonders of the night before all over again, from every angle, in every way, as starved as they had been for each other only hours before. He had thought to close the bedroom door so Oscar didn't walk off with his socks or underwear again.

Ardith had never had a partner like Josh, and he had never been as hungry for any woman as he was for her. They were insatiable, until they had made love so many times that Ardith thought it wasn't possible, and they could hardly move as they lay on her bed.

"Oh my God, Josh, this is insane. I was going to tell you again that you need to be with someone your age or ten years younger, but I don't think I could give this up now. I'm addicted."

"Me too. I think you might kill me. I've never made love that many times in my entire life."

"I've been saving myself for you." She grinned at him, and he laughed, rolled over and kissed her.

"If I'd known it would be like this, I would have put a move on you immediately. I wanted to, but it was pure fantasy," and they both knew this couldn't have happened if Bill hadn't died unexpectedly. She would never have cheated on him, and Josh loved that about her. She was someone you could trust to do the right thing. Everything about this felt right to both of them, except for their age difference, which bothered Ardith but not him. He didn't care if she was a hundred, he loved her just as she was, and she was the sexiest woman he had ever been with. She was a wonderful lover because she loved him. He could tell with everything she did, and he felt the same way about her. It was a precious gift.

"I hope you like watching TV," she said when they got out of bed and went to take a shower together.

"Why?"

"Because if we don't find something else to do for a few hours, I won't be able to sit down for a week."

They showered and then ate the cold chicken Benicia had left for her. There was enough for both, and Ardith wondered if the housekeeper suspected something, but she doubted it. Benicia was just a generous cook.

After they ate, Josh had an idea. He told her to get her purse and refused to tell her where he was taking her. They went in the Range Rover this time, and he drove her to West Hollywood, to a bar where he used to hang out, adjacent to a bowling alley. She laughed when she saw it, and they had fun playing. She wasn't good at it, but she enjoyed it thoroughly, and a few people came over and asked for her autograph, so Ardith and Josh knew they had been seen. But Ardith said she didn't care. She wasn't going to hide with him. They wanted to stay discreet for a while, but she was recognized almost everywhere, so sooner or later their secret would come out, if they stayed together and this wasn't just a fling, which it didn't seem to be. It felt like the real thing. The owner of the bar took a picture of them bowling and laughing, while Josh taught her how to get a firm grip on the ball. They weren't doing anything shocking, so if it wound up in the press, it wouldn't hurt anyone. They left soon after the owner took the picture, just to be sure no one had called the paparazzi. And they went home in good spirits. She had fun with him. Every day was a new adventure with Josh.

When they got home, she went to take a shower and let Josh get a head start reading the script. And she picked up the first pages when she joined him after her shower. An hour later, she put down what she'd read so far and looked at him seriously. Neither of them had finished it yet, but she had read enough to know that it was good, and that the part they were offering him would be a game changer for him. It would put him on the map as a serious actor, and she thought he could do it, with some coaching by a pro to refine his skills.

"You've got to do this," she said in a determined tone. "It's a great part for you. You need to change agents now, before you sign anything, accept the part, and get a coach, and your career will take off like lightning after this."

"You really think I can do it?" He looked scared for a minute, but he loved what he had read too. He sensed that this could be the beginning of the big leagues for him. It was a huge leap, but so was being in love with Ardith Law. He felt as though he could do anything now, with her support and faith in him.

"I know you can. Trust me on this. You've got to take this part. Call your agent tomorrow. And I want you to go and see Joe Ricci. They'll work out the commission if you want to switch."

"I will. I promise." He looked like a little kid as he said it, and she smiled at him.

"I'm so proud of you. And thank God someone finally sent you a decent script." It had only taken ten years for that to happen.

"You're next," Josh said to her.

"Joe thinks he might have a good one for me. He's talking to the producer now. He wants to make sure it's an all-star cast before he sends me the script."

"Wouldn't that be cool if we're both working on movies," Josh said, grinning, and she laughed.

"Yes, my love, that's the whole idea. That's what we're going to do. We're both actors."

"I hate to give up being your errand boy," he said wistfully, "the perks have gotten pretty good lately." He kissed her.

"Behave yourself. I want to finish reading the script." They both went on reading after that and loved the ending. "This is great," she confirmed to him. "It's a go, green light all the way. This is just the beginning," she said, excited for him, and he held her in his arms and kissed her, wondering how it had all happened, and how everything had aligned at the same time. He had the woman of his dreams and the doors to his acting career were slowly opening with quality work, after ten years of crap sci-fi and horror movies. He felt like he had won the lottery, and he lay in bed next to Ardith, smiling broadly.

"What are you looking so happy about?" she asked him. It felt as though they had always shared a bed, he was totally at home next to her, and so was she. And Oscar was sound asleep with his head on Ardith's pillow where he liked to be, snoring softly.

"I'm the luckiest man in the world," Josh said to her. There had been a lot of fast changes in their life in the past few weeks, but all of them for the better. Every time he looked at her he felt as though he had been catapulted through time and landed on a cloud.

"I hope you always feel that way," she said seriously. She wanted to wait and see how he felt about it a year from now, and if he regretted being with a woman her age, instead of someone his own. But even if he did, this was sweet for now, and she wanted to cherish it for as long as it lasted. She knew it was a time she would treasure forever, however it turned out. They were taking a leap of faith and hoping it would turn out well for them both. They knew it would never be sweeter than it was right now.

Even a call from Morgan two weeks later didn't spoil it for them. She called her mother in a fury one morning, when they had just gotten out of bed on a Saturday, and were having breakfast naked in the kitchen since Benicia was off on the weekends, and they had come straight from bed, starving after making love.

"You're going bowling with him now?" were her opening words, and Ardith laughed. Even Morgan couldn't ruin how happy she was.

"Did that wind up in the tabloids?" Ardith asked casually, refusing to get sucked into an argument with Morgan, who was enraged.

"Front page of the *Enquirer*," Morgan confirmed.

"They must be low on real dirt at the moment. Yes, I went bowling with Josh."

"I can see that for myself. You look ridiculous. Doesn't that bother you? Going bowling with your assistant, and Bill barely cold in his grave." It was an added dig to make her mother feel guilty, since Morgan had never cared much about Bill either way.

"I think Bill would understand. He didn't believe in mourning anything for long. He believed that life was for the living and that it's better to go on."

"You can't find something more dignified to do?"

"I had a good time," Ardith said without apology. "And I can't be dignified all the time, Morgan. It would bore me to tears. Josh is single, so am I. We weren't hurting anyone. Maybe you should go bowling sometime too. It might relax you."

"I don't understand you, Mother," Morgan said sharply. "You're the biggest star in the world, the epitome of glamour, and you want to be seen going *bowling*?"

"I'll do it in a ballgown next time, if that makes you feel better. You need to lighten up. You work too hard. Don't lose your sense of humor or your sense of the ridiculous." It was good advice.

"Well, clearly you haven't, if ridiculous is the goal here. In that case, you achieved the desired effect flawlessly." For an instant, Ardith was tempted to tell her that she was in love with Josh, but this wasn't how she wanted to tell her, nor the time. She wanted to pick her moment carefully, if it finally came to that, and if she and Josh stayed together, it would.

"Thanks for the heads-up," Ardith said pleasantly. "Have a nice weekend, lots of love, darling, talk to you soon." She hung up before Morgan could think of anything else unpleasant to say.

"What was that about?" Josh asked Ardith as he set a plate of scrambled eggs down in front of her. He liked cooking for her, and he was a better cook.

"It was Morgan. We made the front page of the *Enquirer* going bowling. I figured the owner of the bar would sell the picture." She didn't look bothered by it and Josh looked at her seriously.

"Are you upset?"

"Not in the least," she said, and he believed her. She didn't look it. She looked blissfully happy and so did he. They had made love as soon as they woke up.

"Did you tell her we were having breakfast naked?"

"I didn't get around to it. I'll tell her next time."

"Good." Even Morgan couldn't spoil the fun they were having, or their joyful days, and waving the specter of Bill hadn't worked either. Ardith was sure that wherever he was now, he was happy for her. She had been a perfect companion to him for a dozen years, but now it was her turn, and she was enjoying it to the fullest with Josh. She had no excuses to make to anyone, and certainly not to her daughter, who had criticized every move she made for the past twenty years. It was time for Morgan to get a life of her own. It was Ardith's time with Josh now, and nothing was going to spoil it for them. Ardith wouldn't let that happen, and neither would Josh. They had both waited a long time for what had come to them now so unexpectedly, and despite the years between them, neither of them wanted to give it up. They wanted to do all they could to protect it. It was beginning to seem real. And Ardith hoped it was.

Chapter 8

When Morgan got back to New York on Monday night after Bill's funeral, she sent Ben a brief text, just to let him know she was home. She got no response, and assumed he was already asleep, since she didn't get back to her apartment till two in the morning. But he didn't respond on Tuesday morning either, which was atypical of her experience with him in the short time since they'd met. He had responded to all her texts immediately until then.

She had back-to-back surgeries on Tuesday, a heavy appointment schedule in the office in the afternoon, and postsurgical patients to check before she went home that night. And she had dinner plans with Ben on Wednesday night. He had been enthusiastic about making plans with her, and exquisitely prompt each time she'd seen him. He wasn't a flake like so many of the men of her own generation whom she'd gone out with. It was hard to take younger men seriously, and she eventually stopped seeing them because they had so little understanding of her demanding schedule and dedication to her work.

Ben was one of the most important anchors and news correspondents in the country and the world, a celebrity, and had enormous responsibilities at the network. His career was far more impressive than hers, and he faced challenges and crises every day. Morgan fully understood that his personal life had to take a back seat to his work. His job was his priority at all times, and hers was equally important to her. They were perfectly suited in that way, so she was certain at first that his silence was due to some world crisis he was dealing with. She didn't push him for an answer to her texts on Monday and Tuesday, out of respect for the pressures she knew he dealt with. But on Wednesday morning, she sent him another brief text, asking about the time of their dinner engagement, and got no response to that either. She realized that he had been silent since she'd last seen him on Sunday morning before she flew to L.A. for Bill's funeral. She hadn't heard from him in three days. Until then, their every contact had been passionate, attentive, prompt, and surprisingly loving for the early stage of their romance.

It had been love at first sight for both of them, which was surprising for a man of Ben's experience and age. He had told her it was a first for him. He had admitted to her that until then, he had been somewhat commitment-phobic, and marriage and babies were no longer an option for him. She wasn't eager for either one, so there was no pressure from her in that direction, and she had told him how disenchanted she had been, and disappointed by men her own age. Their desires and their goals in a relationship, hers and Ben's, seemed to be a perfect match, and she didn't want to upset him now by pressuring him. Relationships were fragile in the early stages, particularly for a man with a work life as full as his.

He never confirmed their dinner plan on Wednesday, and the evening slipped by with no word from him. Morgan sat home, feeling sick over it, and suddenly wondered if he had gotten cold feet about her and the relationship. She couldn't explain his silence to herself, and she had no one to discuss it with to reassure her. She had no intention of telling her mother about him this early in the game. Was she just a game to him? Was this something he did? Lit the world on fire and once the flames of passion were blazing, walked away? Were the chase and the conquest enough, and having achieved them, was she no longer of interest to him? Was he weird or crazy or mean? A thousand possible scenarios played out in her head, and finally, at eleven o'clock Wednesday night, he texted her. "My darling, please, please forgive me. Crisis at work. Will explain. Talk tomorrow. I love you, B." She heaved a huge sigh of relief, and at least she knew he hadn't changed his mind and still loved her.

But then she heard nothing from him on Thursday again, no national crisis had come to light, the president hadn't been shot, and she hadn't seen Ben in four days and had had only one text. She wondered if he was stalling or avoiding her. How big a work crisis could it be and why didn't he call her to explain? She was distracted all day Friday in her office, seeing patients, and feeling down about Ben. She obviously wasn't as "special" or as important to him as he had claimed. She felt like a fool, and maybe she had just been a toy he had played with and tossed away. She had assumed that he would be more reliable because he was so much older, but that obviously was not true. His disappearance all week, except for one text, made no sense, and had begun to seem cruel and confusing. She didn't know what to think.

She had a heavy heart when she went home on Friday evening. Ben called her at seven o'clock while she was making a salad. It had been stressful waiting to hear from him, and she felt leery of him now. Could she trust him or believe him? He had admitted that he dated many women, but had convinced her in a stunningly brief time that she was The One he had been looking for all his life. He had been credible, but maybe it was a line that worked for him, and it had with her. She had believed him, and felt humiliated now that she'd been so gullible. Maybe he was no better than the men she had dated who had either cheated on her or lied to her, or were even less interested in marriage and children and more commitment-phobic than she was.

She was startled when she heard Ben's voice on the phone on Friday evening and didn't know what to say at first. He sounded stressed and harassed.

"You must hate me. I've been buried all week. And I didn't want to see you until I knew when I'd have real time to spend with you. It's been a shit show at work—a lead on an important story fell through on Tuesday night, so I couldn't see you on Wednesday, and I'm leaving for Shanghai tomorrow, and Beijing after that. I'm sorry, Morgan. I got eaten alive this week, it's the nature of the business. We're crisis monitors in the news business." She wanted to believe him, but how long did it take to write a text or call? He had only sent one text and never called. She didn't know if she should forget him or give him another chance, but he wasn't an easy man to forget. She had meant everything she said to him. And she felt torn about him now, and unsure. Maybe it would be wiser to close the door on him before he hurt her seriously. It had been a very upsetting week. She didn't know if this was his style or an aberration. She had no one to talk to about it and advise her. Morgan was inclined to keep her own counsel anyway. She never discussed her personal life with anyone, or the brief romances she had, which generally went nowhere. And he was even more private than she was, since he had his fame and reputation to consider. But her heart was on the line here.

She felt on unequal ground because he was famous and so much older. He was in control of their relationship right from the beginning, which was something she tried to avoid too. She didn't like having her fate in other people's hands. And she had slept with him faster than she normally would because he had won her trust so quickly. Now she wanted to take it back, or thought she should. He had demonstrated to her all week that he was unreliable, and she wanted to heed the warning. Her head was telling her to run, and her heart was aching, so soon after their relationship had begun.

"I'm so sorry," he said to her again, sounding contrite, "I shouldn't have stayed silent, but I didn't have a free minute to see you. I missed you all week. I was longing to see you." He sounded so believable, so sorry and sincere, and so vulnerable that she wanted to believe him. "And I hate that I'm leaving tomorrow. I know this is awful, but I just got out of my last briefing before the trip. I need to pack and get some papers together, but is there any chance you'd come over tonight and spend a few hours with me before I leave tomorrow? I hate doing this to you, but I *need* to see you. You're the air I breathe, and

I've been without oxygen without you all week." His eloquence and urgency made him hard to resist and dissolved everything negative she'd thought about him all week. She felt like a puddle at his feet.

"It was a hard week," she said hesitantly, "not knowing what was going on. I like information. Except for one text, you disappeared." She didn't want to close the door on him, if his feelings for her were sincere, but what if they weren't?

"It was a hard week for me too," he said immediately. "I missed you incredibly." He sounded urgent and sexy when he said it. "How was your stepfather's funeral?"

"Full of pomp and ceremony. All of Old Hollywood was there. I left after the burial and didn't stay for the reception. My mother wasn't happy about it, but I had to get back. I had surgery the next day." The demands of her own job were pressing too, which made her willing to understand and forgive the pressure he lived with on a daily basis, if he would explain it to her and not vanish. Silence was not golden in this case.

"At least you went. I'm constantly put in situations like that too. Most people don't understand it. They're selfish and expect you to meet their needs, when my work life makes it impossible to meet everyone's needs." She didn't want to be one of the selfish people and appear needy and grasping to him. Now that they had found each other, she wanted to be a support and a comfort to him, not a burden. She was trying to be undemanding, and she also needed a fair exchange. She was beginning to see that she might have to be needless to be with him, available when he was, and tolerant and uncomplaining when he couldn't be free for her, like that week. His circumstances were so special that she wondered if she'd have to be extra accommodating. Ben was no ordinary human, he was a very special man, with a high-level job of international importance. He wasn't the president, or curing cancer, but he was the most important anchor in the business. Allowances had to be made if one aspired to be with him, and he had already complained to her that women never understood it, so his involvement with them ended if they expected him to attend their office Christmas party, their sister's birthday, or their son's, or make a baby. That was the last thing he needed in a life as stressful as his, and he didn't tolerate it. Morgan didn't want to disqualify herself this early and was trying to be different from the others. She wanted to be everything he needed, and was willing to put aside her own needs in the process. But he could have texted or called her, and he didn't. It wasn't a lot to expect, and she'd had a miserable week because of him. He didn't seem to understand how sad he had made her, and how discouraged she'd been, and even worried about him.

"I know it sounds like shit, but would you be willing to forgive me and come over around nine or ten tonight? I'll have everything done and out of the way by then. I could be with you until noon tomorrow, Morgan. It would mean the world to me if you'd come over. I'd come to you, if you'll have me, but I can stay with you longer if I leave from my place. The car is coming for me at noon for the trip to China." She hesitated for an instant, and decided to give him another chance and accept the time he was offering her. It was on his timetable, but his leaving for Shanghai the next day meant there was no other choice, and hopefully they would negotiate a better system of communication in future. It crossed her mind that in some ways, this was a last-minute booty call, but you couldn't call it that with a man of his stature. Ben was a world-famous, award-winning, international celebrity with a major job based on world crises and an unpredictable schedule. If she loved him, she'd have to get used to it, and share what time he could spare for her.

"I'll come over," she said calmly, her voice devoid of reproach. She forgave him for the painful silence he had put her through and was willing to see him with a clean slate. It was a decision she made knowingly, aware of the risk she was taking with her heart. He might break it.

"I adore you, darling. I'll send a car for you. I'll have him there at nine-thirty. I can't wait to see you."

"Me too," Morgan said, smiling for the first time all week. It had been agonizing waiting to hear from him. It didn't seem like a lot now, only five days since she'd last seen him, she reminded herself, but the uncertainty of it had been brutal. She had felt sick about it all week, and it had gotten worse every day. His call that night had been an unexpected gift which had washed the pain away, put balm on the wound, and finally offered some meager explanation. His single text all week had not been enough for her.

"Thank God you're willing to forgive me and give me another chance," he said, relieved. "I was afraid you wouldn't and I'd blown it. I love you."

"I love you too," she said softly. "I'll see you later. Can I bring you anything? Have you eaten?" She wanted to take care of him, be the loving woman in his life, who brought him sustenance and comfort. It was all she had to give him. He had everything else.

"All I need is you," he said warmly.

She was going to have fourteen hours with Ben before he left on a trip where he would be running constantly in different time zones on the other side of the world, and she doubted that she'd hear much from him while he met with world leaders and covered international crises. So, the fourteen hours would be that much more important and precious, giving her emotional food to draw on until he returned, and hopefully making up for the stressful week he had just given her. It was a lifestyle, Morgan realized now, she might have to get used to if she wanted to be with him. She thought she did. He was different and exciting, world-famous and important, and he loved her. He wasn't some run-of-the-mill banker or lawyer or doctor who went to an office every day and came home at night and never did anything extraordinary or outstanding. He was a star of major proportions, and she told herself that one had to make allowances for men like him. He was head and shoulders above any man she'd ever known, and fame was not entirely unfamiliar to her because of her mother. She knew that one had to make exceptions for stars, although she had made few for her mother and had held her to normal standards. She didn't want to do that with Ben. She was willing to be generous and forgiving, in ways she had never been with her mother. But she was in love with Ben, which made it all different, in her mind.

The car came for her promptly at nine-thirty, and drove her to Central Park West. There was little traffic at that hour on a Friday night, and it took fifteen minutes to head west and cross the park. The doorman buzzed Ben's apartment, and after speaking to Ben, sent her up immediately. Ben was waiting for her in the doorway in a black turtleneck sweater and black jeans and short black Hermès boots, and he was impeccably groomed. Without a word, he pulled her into his arms, held her tightly, took her breath away when he kissed her, and then led her into his elegant, beautifully decorated apartment and closed the door behind her. He looked like a man she had just saved from drowning, and she was glad she had come. She knew that others who didn't know him might say it was a booty call, but she knew better now. They were sharing the little time he had for himself before he left on an important mission. What he did was of world importance, not just an ordinary job like hers, or those of other men she knew. She felt very small when she was with him. He was an enormous persona, and he had invited her into his private world, which made her feel very special. She had never felt that way before with any man. Ben made her feel like a princess, a princess he hadn't called or texted all week. She tried to remind herself to keep her feet on the ground, and forgot instantly.

Ben had a bottle of Dom Pérignon champagne chilling for her and poured her a glass as soon as she took her coat off. She had worn gray slacks and a new white cashmere sweater, with her long blond hair straight down her back. She didn't have to look serious and medical for him, and the fact that she was a highly skilled surgeon was irrelevant in his world. No one knew her name. The entire world, and every head of state, knew who he was. And the twenty-five-year age gap between them added to his gravitas and her respect for him. He knew so much more about life, the world, and delicate political situations she could only guess at.

As he had promised, he had everything done and put away when Morgan arrived. He turned his full attention on her, sat down on the couch next to her, and drank the champagne with her. She felt its effect with the second glass, as he kissed her, and slowly undressed her, and they were in his bed minutes later, soaring to heights only he was able to bring her to. She felt like a novice at everything when she was with Ben. He was so worldly and so wise and so sophisticated, and so tender and loving. Morgan felt as though he pulled her into heaven with him, after having been in hell all week without any word from him. Now she was back in the magic world he shared with her when she was with him.

They made love for hours, and she finally fell asleep with his arms around her. She didn't know if it was him or the champagne, but she felt as though she was floating as she drifted off to sleep, feeling safe in his arms.

He handed her a black silk pajama top of his to wear to breakfast the next morning, and cooked an omelet as he made her laugh and told her stories about previous trips to China.

"I'd like to take you with me one day, if that slave driver you work for and I went to school with will give you the time off. In fact, I have an interview set up with the French president in a few weeks, and I'd like you to come with me. It would be a good chance for you to meet Amanda, my daughter."

"How will she feel about us?" Morgan asked him thoughtfully, as she ate the delicious omelet he had cooked for her.

"She'll be crazy about you," Ben said confidently.

"I'm only three years older than she is, that might bother her," Morgan said, and Ben looked unimpressed. He smiled when he answered her.

"I warned you I've had a bit of a checkered career since I've been divorced. I've gone out with women much younger than both of you on occasion. It was always a huge mistake for obvious reasons, but I think Amanda will be relieved that you're closer to her age, even a few years older, and not some groupie young enough to be my granddaughter. You've made me respectable again. Or I've grown up, I suppose. I have no patience for the young ones anymore. I've given that up."

"I hope you won't miss it," Morgan teased him, feeling powerful and safe after making love with him all night. He had put her doubts to rest and made her comfortable again. She was glad she had spent the night with him. It had erased the painful week from her mind. He was easy to forgive when she was in his arms.

After breakfast, they took a bath together in his enormous black marble bathtub. Everything in his apartment was beautiful, masculine, and elegantly designed, while still being functional and comfortable. He pointed out a small dressing room with closets where she could leave some clothes when he came back, which made her feel welcome and at home. He obviously wasn't avoiding commitment with her, or intimacy.

He traveled in a suit and an overcoat, all in black, with a single suitcase and his briefcase, and shortly before noon, he took her in his arms again.

"I hate to leave you, Morgan. I'll be back in ten days. Try not to forget me while I'm gone." He looked as though he meant it and she was touched.

"I'll try not to." There was no way she could ever forget Ben, or the time she spent with him. He was a universe away and better than any man she'd ever known, even with his complicated work life.

"I'm not the easiest man to put up with," he said humbly. "I'll try to be better. You make me want to be the best I can ever be, in every-thing."

"You're doing fine," she said, and kissed him tenderly. She was already longing for him again before he left, and he was still hungry for her too. They left his apartment together with regret.

"I'll be back soon," he reminded her, and kissed her passionately again before the elevator came. He had already explained to her that cell service and internet would be irregular in many of the places he was going, and the time difference would make it even more difficult to call her. "And try to get the time off to come to Paris with me," he said to her in the car. He kept his fingers tightly laced in hers all the way to her apartment, and kissed her long and hard before she got out. He dropped her off, so his driver could take the East River Drive toward the airport, and she stood in front of her building and watched him pull away. Every ounce of her was his—in fourteen hours, he had stolen her heart again. All her fears of the previous days had vanished. She felt sure of him again, excited about the future, and proud to be with him. She felt as though she had been born to be with him, and he said the same.

He texted her on the way to the airport, and she read it with a smile. "You own me, Morgan Walker. I love you. B." She couldn't ask for more reassurance than that. She had forgiven him for the past week.

Chapter 9

The glow of being with Ben for those magical fourteen hours before he left stayed with Morgan for several days. He had warned her that he probably wouldn't be able to contact her while he was gone, and he was true to his word. But she wasn't worried about it this time. He had told her what to expect, and his silence didn't seem ominous. She was looking toward the future, and had asked for the time off to go to Paris with him, and was granted a week off. None of her partners were planning to be away then, and she scheduled her patients accordingly.

Morgan was still coasting on the time she had spent with Ben before he left when the senior partner, Dr. Andrew Scott, called her into his office five days after Ben left for China. He looked serious when she walked into his office, and she was suddenly worried that she had committed some medical error she wasn't aware of, or maybe a patient had complained to him about their result. Plastic surgery was a delicate business involving psychological issues as much as medical ones, which Morgan and her partners were sensitive to and well aware of.

"Come in, Morgan," Andrew Scott invited her when she knocked on his office door after he had summoned her. He seemed more serious than usual as she sat down across from him. He hesitated for a minute and then waded into what he feared could be deep waters, but he felt he couldn't ignore what he'd been told, for several reasons. "I don't usually pay attention to gossip, but I want to address a matter with you which came to my attention in a roundabout way, outside the office. I don't know if there's any truth to it, but you've been very successful in the partnership, and I wouldn't like you to jeopardize that."

"I hope I haven't committed a medical error of some kind," she said seriously.

"Not a medical error, but perhaps an ethical one. I actually heard it from a school friend who mentioned it to me casually. There might not even be any truth to it, and if that's the case, I apologize in advance for listening to stable talk." Andrew smiled at her then for the first time. "I think you're aware that Ben Ryan and I attended Harvard together, a long time ago. I ran into his college roommate the other day, who seemed to have the impression that Ben is currently involved with one of my partners, which doesn't take Sherlock Holmes to figure out. You're our only female partner, so it could only be you. And you saw him as one of my patients for a surgical follow-up while I was away. We don't have rules about that, or stringent policies. I prefer to allow wisdom to be our guideline, but we don't look favorably on the partners dating our patients, if it can be avoided, and ordinarily, it can. It can lead to some awkward situations we prefer to avoid.

"Ben Ryan is a brilliant, appealing, charming man, and I lost the attention of more than one young woman to him when we were at Harvard together. He was tough to compete with, even then, and more so now. So I understand Ben's appeal to most women. Generally, we would prefer it if you don't date the patients. I can't forbid it, but I strongly advise you against it." Morgan nodded agreement.

"He took me by surprise," she said honestly, wanting to clear the air with her senior partner. "He was very persistent about it, and very charming. I'll admit I thought maybe I could have dinner with him just that once. And I have seen him again, and we intend to continue seeing each other. I don't believe it's frivolous, and it's turned out to be more serious than we expected, but we've been very discreet, and will continue being so. I'm truly sorry if it's caused you concern and it's awkward."

"I know how convincing he is," Andrew Scott said fairly. "There's no man on the planet more charming than Ben is when he wants something. I just wouldn't want to see a similar situation arise again, or to have you make a habit of dating patients. You're a very attractive woman, and I'm sure many of our patients would like to take advantage of it. Only Ben has the guts to do it," he said with a smile.

"I certainly wouldn't date any other patients," Morgan assured him, "and no one has ever asked." He had always noticed that Morgan maintained a cool professional demeanor with the patients and he had never been concerned before.

"I appreciate that," Andrew said, and paused. "And on a more personal note, I will venture where angels fear to tread, out of concern for you, as a partner and a friend. I'm very fond of Ben, we've been friends for a long time, but he has a predilection for complicated relationships with women which don't always turn out well. I've seen him leave a trail of broken hearts behind him for many years, and I don't want yours to be one of them. He had two disastrous marriages with women who don't speak well of him. Ben has a way of creating emotional drama. I don't want you to get hurt by him, particularly because he's my friend and you met him here. Be careful, Morgan. He's a complex man, more than he appears. I shouldn't even say that much, but when I heard that he was dating you, I was concerned. He lives on the edge of danger in his professional life, and his personal life seems to follow the same path."

"I appreciate your concern," Morgan said calmly. "He himself acknowledges that he's gotten into some difficult and even unwise situations. He claims that he's grown up." She smiled at her partner. "And everything seems to be going smoothly so far," she reassured him.

"I'm relieved to hear it. Ben has always invited drama all around him. That doesn't seem your style."

"It isn't, and my eyes are wide open," but so was her heart, she realized, and didn't admit to her partner. "We'll see what happens. He's in China right now."

"He's a brilliant man, with an incredible talent. Maybe men like him are always complicated. He's not earthbound like the rest of us. Men like him are always dazzling, but they can be dangerous if your heart is involved."

"Thank you," Morgan said simply, touched by his concern and advice. He was the same age as Ben, and she knew the senior partner had twin daughters about her age. One of them was divorced, so he wasn't unfamiliar with the romantic issues of young women. The divorced twin was in advertising, and the married one was an obstetrician with three children of her own. Andrew Scott was a family man with four adult children he was close to, and had been married for forty years. He was everything Morgan admired in a man, and she wished she had had a father like him. But Ben Ryan was a star, and the same rules didn't apply to stars, and one had to make allowances for them. She could tell that Andrew was fond of him, but he was leery of him too. He never mentioned the age difference, but she was sure it was a factor. Twenty-five years was a big age gap, and Andrew probably wouldn't have liked it for his girls. Ben was not every father's dream, but he was hers, for now. She hoped it would last, and that she wouldn't be one of the trail of broken hearts Andrew Scott had referred to, but anything was possible. She had faith in Ben, but she had seen enough of life and been out with enough men to know that things didn't always turn out well. The wide age gap between them led her to hope that Ben was more mature than any man she'd known till now.

Morgan left her partner's office a few minutes later, feeling warned, slightly chastised, but confident. Andrew was less so. He knew Ben too well, and too many of the women he had hurt, badly, not just minor dating casualties. Ben had done a lot of damage to the women he loved, particularly the two he had married, who had always been very vocal about how much they hated him, and how badly he had behaved to them. Morgan was an innocent in that world, Andrew knew, and he just hoped she wouldn't be Ben's next victim, and that he was honest when he said he had grown up. He had always been a dangerous man to love until then. Andrew had tried to warn her, which was all he could do. The rest was up to her, and maybe Ben had reformed. Andrew hoped so, as he had great respect and affection for his young partner, and thought she deserved a good man. He wasn't sure that Ben was it. And based on past history, Andrew believed he wasn't. All he could hope was that Morgan wasn't in over her head. When it came to women, Ben was a pro, and had been all his life.

Ben didn't contact Morgan from Shanghai, Singapore, or Beijing. He spent a single night in Hong Kong and sent her a text that said only "Missing you. love, B." which told her nothing of substance, but at least she was on his mind and he had contacted her. She sent him an answering text that he didn't respond to, which no longer surprised her. His trip ended in London, and he could easily have written to her from there, but he didn't. She knew the day he was due back, and he didn't contact her then either. She wasn't sure if his trip had been extended, or if he was busy when he got back. She heard nothing from him for four more days. She hadn't seen him in two weeks by then. It was then that she saw the photograph of Josh and her mother bowling on the cover of the *Enquirer* that irritated her so much. She was already tense, waiting to hear from Ben. She had had only the one brief text from him in the two weeks he'd been gone. She wasn't afraid of other women, although it was a possibility. It was more about his remaining distant and detached when it suited him, with no thought of how his silences affected her. Were they dating or not?

Or was she just a booty call? She had fallen prey to his charm every time, and accepted all his explanations and excuses.

She finally heard from Ben at midnight five days after he got back. He sounded exhausted and said it had been a rough trip. He didn't ask her to come over that night.

"Are you all right?" Morgan asked him, concerned. She had run out of explanations for his silences.

"More or less," he said cryptically. "I have a lot going on." He didn't say if it was personal or due to work, and she was afraid to ask. They had allegedly been dating for four weeks, and she had had two elegant dinners out with him, a weekend of unforgettable sex in his apartment before she left for Bill's funeral, and a night of unbridled passion—which did seem more like a booty call now—before his trip to China. Ben was always seeing her at the eleventh hour, on short notice, and the sex was fabulous. He seemed so loving each time they met, and what he said to her indicated that he had never experienced anything like it and that Morgan was the woman he had searched high and low for all his life and finally found. But then he would disappear again, and all the same doubts would bob to the surface in his silence. He was so convincing when she was with him, and terrifying when he wasn't. She was never sure if she could trust him with her heart or not. His being so much older than she was somehow gave her the impression that he was solid and trustworthy, that she could count on him. But could she?

Once they were apart, she always had the feeling that she didn't know what was going on. Was he simply overburdened at work, or did he have a whole other life she knew nothing about and fitted her in when it suited him? Much as Morgan hated to admit it, their whole relationship for the past month had been like an ongoing booty call, which wasn't what she wanted with Ben. The sex was fabulous, but it wasn't enough. It acted like a drug, lulling her into a sense of security that dissipated as soon as he was gone. And what she couldn't figure out was whether he was real. Or was he just playing with her?

All of it ran through her mind when he finally called her at midnight, and she was braced to refuse him if he invited her to come over at that hour, but he didn't. He startled her with the tone of his voice and what he said. There was an urgency to it, and it sounded ominous.

"Can you come over tomorrow night?" he asked her. But there was nothing romantic about his tone. It sounded as though something was wrong. "We have to talk." All her warning signals and alarms went off when he said it. She didn't dare ask him what it was about, the age factor played into it again, and she never dared call him on the carpet as she would have a younger man. Ben wasn't someone you called to task. He played life on his terms. She had already understood that.

"I can come over," she said in a neutral tone.

"Six o'clock?"

"I'm seeing my last patient at five-thirty."

"Seven then. And Morgan . . ." There was a pause. "I'm sorry I've been out of touch again. I couldn't help it. I love you. I hope you know that." She wanted to believe him but wasn't sure she did.

"I love you too, Ben," she said softly, trying not to soften too much at his words and lower her guard entirely. "See you tomorrow." As they hung up, all she could remember were Andrew Scott's words, telling her that Ben was a complicated man who had left a trail of broken hearts behind him. She hoped it wouldn't be true for her.

Chapter 10

Morgan spent a long, anxious day seeing patients before she met Ben at his apartment the day after he finally called her at midnight. All she could think of were the various possible scenarios to induce him to say that they "had to talk." Either he had decided he didn't want a serious relationship with her after all, or she had stepped over the line in some way which disqualified her as the love of his life, or there was another woman he had failed to mention to her, or he had a serious illness and he didn't want to inflict it on her, or he was being transferred to another country or city and couldn't see the sense of a long-distance relationship with her. Anything was possible, and with a life and career as complex as Ben's, he could have reached any number of negative conclusions about her in the last two weeks. Maybe he had come to his senses and wanted to stop seeing her.

Morgan went straight to Ben's apartment from the office when her last patient left, and she didn't go home to change. She was wearing a navy skirt and sweater set and looked professional with her hair in a sleek bun. He was wearing jeans, a black shirt, and black suede loafers, and looked like the sexy, handsome star he was, which she tried to ignore when he opened the door to her. But he hugged her so tightly and kissed her so hard that she no longer thought he had invited her over to break up with her. She couldn't guess what it was that they had to talk about.

He was drinking vodka on the rocks, and she accepted a glass of wine, to help her relax. They made small talk for a few minutes, and he kissed her again. She didn't know if she should stop him or not. She had no idea what was in store and had dreaded the conversation all day. She had had to force herself to concentrate on what her last patient said. All she could think about was Ben and their meeting after work.

It was the first time she had seen him since his trip to China and England, and he had already been home for six days without seeing her, which she didn't think was a good sign. He had clearly not been eager to see her, no matter how hard he kissed her when he finally did. She wasn't sure if the passionate kiss was due to fear, despera tion, or guilt for what he was about to say to her. He was constantly unpredictable and contact with him was irregular. She never knew when she'd hear from him or see him again.

He dragged his feet to start the conversation and Morgan finally broached it with him.

"So, what's this about?" She tried not to sound aggressive or men acing. Ben looked nervous as he stared at his feet, and then took a long swallow of his drink. He looked straight at Morgan then, and she felt the same quiver in her stomach that she felt every time she saw him. Just being near him gave her a thrill. She hoped it didn't show, she was trying to appear neutral and unconcerned. It was the opposite of what she felt, which was raw fear, if he was about to break up with her. It didn't seem that way, but she wasn't sure. It was so often a guessing game with him.

"It's about my past coming back to haunt me," Ben said miserably. He had the look of a boy in the headmaster's office, instead of the self-assured star that he was.

"I expected a certain amount of that," she said calmly, in her best surgeon's voice. The voice of wisdom and experience that would encourage people to put their lives in her hands. She did it well, but this was different, although he smiled nervously as he looked at her. "I didn't think you were a saint or had been living in a monastery before we met. We all have skeletons in the distant past."

"That's good to know," he teased her, and then grew serious again. "Unfortunately, I'm not talking about the distant past. It's more recent than that."

"How recent?" Morgan asked him, frowning.

"Very recent. Around the same time I met you, right before. They hired a young intern at the office. I have no idea what she was supposed to do. Make coffee, file, serve cookies, whatever. Most of them are young and not very attractive. This one was a hot little thing, with a come-hither look. She flirted with all the guys, she wore miniskirts and tight sweaters. I'd been working on a story for two weeks straight, with no sleep. They sent me a file I was looking for, I was working from home, and she delivered it. She did everything she could to entice me. I swear, I wasn't after her, I was blind tired and I barely looked at her. I had to send some papers back to the office signed, and she waited for me to sign them. She sat on the couch with her legs apart. After a while she lay down and said she was tired, and her shirt was half unbuttoned. I was tired but I'm not dead, for chrissake." He looked stressed as he told Morgan the story.

"Please don't tell me she's sixteen years old and you're going to jail for rape," Morgan said with a knot in her stomach, and he shook his head.

"She's twenty-two, an adult. I left the room to get another file, and when I came back she had her shirt off and she was sitting there bare-chested with her tits out. I thought I was hallucinating. I had no intention of laying a hand on her. I know better, in this day and age. She propositioned me. She said she's been in love with me since she was thirteen, and all she wanted was to have sex with me once. Maybe I was flattered, or tired, or nuts. She walked over and put her hands on me, and I resisted at first. She was very enticing. I asked her how old she was, and she told me. I wasn't seeing anyone, I hadn't met you yet, and I figured the fates had served her to me on a silver platter. I shouldn't have done it. It was stupid and wrong. I didn't rape her. I had sex with her. Most guys would have. She was hot. We had sex. She went back to the office two hours later, and I figured that was it. I figured I'd never see her again. She had a four-week internship. She was young and cute. And then I met you. And like some kind of evil karma, she started calling me. I told her it had been a mistake, that it was an unfortunate slip on both our parts, she needs to find someone her own age. She was more than willing to have sex, she lured me into it. I was a fool. She got pissed when I wouldn't see her again. She showed up at my apartment a couple of times and I didn't let her in. I only had sex with her that once. That's all. It was the mistake of the century. She emailed me when I was in China."

"I thought you didn't have internet," Morgan interrupted him.

"I did in Hong Kong. She said I had to call her, it was urgent. I didn't like the sound of it, so I did. She's blackmailing me. I've had stalkers before, and a few angry women, but nothing like this. She says she's pregnant. She wants me to support her, acknowledge the baby, and marry her, and if I don't, she's going to claim I threatened and coerced her and raped her, and if a jury believes her, I'll probably go to prison. I've never had a MeToo claim against me. I swear. I've never coerced or raped anyone. I've had sex with consenting women, a lot of them, all satisfied customers when we parted company, except my ex-wives who were greedy. But that was about money, not blackmail, and I paid them handsomely. I'm not going to marry this girl, it's out of the question. If the baby really is mine, I'll support it. But I'm not going to have her or the baby in my life, and I'm not going to marry her. And I have no defense against the claim that I raped her. I have no proof that I didn't. And she's pregnant, so if the baby is mine, that's evidence that we had sex, and she can claim I raped her and got her pregnant."

"Does she have proof that you did rape her? Any kind of testimony, or evidence?" Morgan asked him in a dead voice. She hadn't expected a story like the one he told her, which was a lot more than "complicated." It was unsavory, but it was the kind of thing that could happen. He was free, single, and not involved with Morgan at the time. But it was a stupid thing to do, and he knew it too, and he regretted it bitterly. And Morgan believed him. He looked miserable.

"There's no evidence that I know of," he answered, looking distraught. "And it was only that one time. Then I met you, we fell in love, and I never saw her again. It happened right before I met you. I never intended to see her again anyway. I didn't call you when I got back from London because I've been upset. I've been seeing my lawyer every day to make a plan. We can contact the police and accuse her of extortion, but I have no proof of that. All of her threats have been by phone. But if the network hears about it and believes her, or a jury, I'll be out of a job. A big job. She can destroy me with a MeToo claim. If she wins, I'll be out of work and unemployable, and I may even have fathered a child I don't want with a girl I don't even know. I've been too stressed to call you or see you. I figured you might not want anything to do with me with all this going on. But I think you should know. The next few months are going to be rough."

"Are you sure she's pregnant? She may have cooked that up to scare you and give her some leverage," Morgan said calmly.

"She sent me some pregnancy test that showed positive, but who knows where she got it. She sent it when I got home."

"You can get a prenatal DNA test to prove if the baby is yours, if there is one," Morgan said practically, sounding like a doctor now.

"Is that true?" Ben looked relieved. "My lawyer thought so too. He was going to check it out."

"If she isn't pregnant, and/or the baby isn't yours, I think you could bring charges of extortion against her. And if she has no proof of rape, it could all be cooked up. She may not be pregnant at all, or she may already have been pregnant by someone else when she slept with you. The whole thing could have been a setup. She must have figured you'd demand a DNA test, though."

"I think she figured I wouldn't want to risk a scandal and getting fired on a MeToo charge. Nothing like this has ever happened to me." There was a frantic look in his eyes. She could see that he was scared.

"It sounds like you've been lucky until now," Morgan said quietly. She didn't like the story he had told her, but she almost felt sorry for him, if everything he said was true. With his promiscuous practices before her, he had been an easy victim for a girl like the intern.

"I hated to tell you and I would understand if you wanted nothing more to do with me. Even if I come out of this innocent, it will be a scandal for a while. And if the baby is mine, it will be embarrassing for both of us. For me, and for you by association."

"I don't care, as long as you're innocent," she said simply. "And if the baby is yours, if you're not involved with her you'll have to deal with it, and I think I can live with it. You're not the first man who's wound up with a paternity suit after a one-night stand. It's unfortunate and it will cost you, but I'm not completely naïve, I'm a doctor. I can fix you up with someone reliable to do the DNA test if you want." She was being remarkable about it, and Ben looked shaken and grateful.

"I don't imagine your mother will appreciate a story like this, if we ever get that far, and I meet her."

"She's a grown-up, she's heard stories like this before. Men who sleep around are vulnerable to it, and so are famous men," Morgan said with a sigh.

"I promise you, Morgan, it was only that one time, before I met you. And she taught me a lesson. I've reformed, there are no free rides. My lawyer convinced me of that this week. We're going to demand a pregnancy test by a doctor we choose, and I'll remind him to ask the doctor about the prenatal DNA test."

"I think it can be done very early in the pregnancy," Morgan said. "It's not my specialty so I don't know the timing. And if she lied about the pregnancy or your paternity, then I don't suppose the accusation of rape will hold much water."

"I hope the network thinks so. She could cost me my job. If I agree to support her and the baby, she'll drop the rape charges. She wants a fortune."

"She's an ambitious girl," Morgan said, and Ben put an arm around her.

"Do you think you could ever forgive me for this mess? It's a hell of a way for us to start out, and I don't want to lose you."

"I can't say that I love it," she admitted, "but hopefully you can resolve it quickly, either because she's lying all the way down the line and the baby isn't yours, or if it is, you'll come to a fast agreement with her, so you don't have to deal with her after that. Does the network know?" she asked him.

"Not yet. I was panicked when she told me what she has in mind."

"I'll call one of my OB friends tomorrow and get a test set up," she offered, and he nodded. "I hope it's not yours, that would be a lot simpler. She sounds like a liar to me, and that's a pretty lucky shot if she got pregnant on one try, but it happens. I can assume you didn't wear a condom?" He looked guilt-ridden when she asked.

"I was lazy and stupid, and I'd had a couple of drinks."

"Yes, you were stupid," she readily agreed. "You should probably

get an HIV test too," for her protection as well. He had worn a condom with her, but she had insisted. He was too old to be as irrespon-
sible as he had been, but what was done was done. She hoped he
wasn't having a baby with another woman, but if he had no attachment to her, and no relationship, the damage could be contained, if
he paid the girl enough and supported the baby. He would be paying
penance forever for it. She was stunned by the stupidity of men
sometimes, and the naivete, even at Ben's age.

"Do you hate me?"

"No." She smiled a small wintry smile at him. "Let's just get you
out of this without your getting fired or going to prison on MeToo
charges. The baby is almost the least of it." But all combined it was
sordid.

Ben had another drink then and poured her more wine. "You're
an amazing woman, Morgan. I was an idiot to have sex with her.
Those days are over for me now." She hoped it was true, but it had
only been weeks ago, and it was too recent to believe in his total
reformation. That would bear watching, and the encounter had happened before they met, although not long before. "I don't suppose
you'd stay here tonight, would you?" He had the pleading eyes of a
schoolboy when he asked her, but the confessional meeting had gone
better than he had hoped. She was practical and down-to-earth, and
was willing to stand by him, if what he told her was true. She
wouldn't have if he had raped the girl, but she didn't think he would.
She believed him. And the girl sounded like the worst kind of gold-
digger to a criminal degree. If she was pregnant by him, she had
won the lottery, which she had probably been hoping for. Maybe she
even knew she was ovulating, that was easy to detect now. If nothing

else, she was an opportunist, and he had been a fool and a willing victim.

"I might," she said in answer to his question about spending the night. She had missed him for two weeks, although this wasn't the reunion she had dreamed of.

He was so relieved by her sensible reaction and seeming willingness to forgive that he wanted to make love to her and spend the night with her. As much as the girl, he was worried about his job. Corporations were quick to react to MeToo scandals now, but he had a flawless reputation. He had an active sex life but had never raped or coerced anyone. And no one had ever accused him of threats or force, until now.

He kissed her, and minutes later, as their passion mounted, they wound up in his bedroom, making love. It had all the fervor of make-up sex, and his terror about his situation fueled his desire for her. He had dropped a bomb on her, and Morgan didn't like the idea of his making love with someone else. But he wasn't a virgin, and she believed it had been before he met her, and it only proved that people made mistakes at any age, even sixty-three. Responsible men of her own generation were more careful about protection, to avoid disease and a mess like the one he was in now, but they made mistakes too. And men of his generation were famous for being careless. They had come into their sexual independence in another era, with fewer STDs, and when the pill was the answer to their prayers to avoid pregnancy. Nowadays, it was more complicated.

Despite her dislike of his situation, Morgan spent the night with him, and it was warm and tender, and as sensual and passionate as before.

She went straight to her office in the morning and called a friend who was an OB in a practice she referred patients to. They had gone to medical school together.

"How's my favorite plastic surgeon?" Perry Blackstone asked when she called him, and she explained the problem, in a slightly sanitized version. She didn't say it was for a man she was in love with. "How pregnant is the girl?" he asked Morgan.

"I'm not sure, somewhere around six weeks, I think."

"They'll have to wait another two weeks. The most reliable test we've got can only be done after eight weeks. It's ninety-nine percent accurate."

"How fast are the results?"

"Seven business days for the lab."

"Thanks, Perry. I'll tell my friend."

"Let's have dinner sometime," he suggested.

"I'd love that." She and Perry had been good friends at school, but she rarely saw him now. They were both busy.

"I'm on call three nights a week. It's a small practice. Four nights sometimes. I'm free the other nights."

"No girlfriend at the moment?" she asked. She and he had never dated and were just friends.

"No. OBs make shit boyfriends, I'm told. They're always on call, delivering babies. I'm sure your life is a lot more civilized, doing face-lifts and nose jobs and Botox shots."

"My hours are better than yours, but what you do is probably more fun."

"Sometimes. Tell your friend to give me a call in a couple of weeks and we'll run the DNA test. It just takes a few minutes, the time of a blood draw or saliva test for him."

"I'll have him call you," she promised, and called Ben afterward with the information.

"What if she refuses the DNA test?" he asked, sounding panicked.

"Then you know she's lying for sure, and we kill her," Morgan said, and he laughed. "And you bring charges of extortion."

"This is not going to be fun," Ben said, still sounding tense and very worried, but Morgan had been wonderful so far. "What about Paris? Will you still come?"

"Yes," she said firmly. She was steady as a rock. And despite the mess he was in, she trusted him. "I got the time off. We might as well use it." And they'd face whatever came after that.

"I'll call my lawyer about the DNA test," Ben said.

"My med school friend said it'll only take a few minutes, and you'll have the results in seven business days."

"I hope she'll agree to it."

"She has no choice if she's telling the truth and she thinks it's yours. That test is the only thing that will validate her story or kill it. It's ninety-nine percent accurate and she can do it in two weeks."

"That's perfect timing, when we come back from Paris," he said. He'd been looking forward to the trip, and she was too, although there would be a level of tension now, waiting to come home and do the DNA test. Ben's lawyer was going to deliver the message to the young woman's lawyer that his accuser had to do the test, or they would go to the police and bring charges of extortion against her. It was hardball time now, and Ben had a tough lawyer. Given who he was, Ben was a target. He had played a dangerous game when he had sex with the intern. "See you tonight?" Ben asked Morgan before he hung up, and she smiled.

"Yeah, that would be nice," she said, and hurried off to see her first patient, and Ben closed his eyes and prayed that Tracy McCarthy's baby wasn't his, and that the DNA test would save his life and his job.

Chapter 11

Once Ardith told Josh how good she thought the script was, the wheels were set in motion. He went to meet Joe Ricci, Ardith's agent, who signed him as a client and negotiated the deal for him for the movie and a split commission arrangement with Josh's previous agent. Josh was pleasantly surprised by how much they paid him, and they had lined up a strong cast he was excited to work with. Joe hired a drama coach for him, and Josh worked with him every day, went to the gym every morning to get back in shape, and still spent several hours a day helping Ardith with projects she needed assistance with.

She was excited about the script Joe had given her too. There were still a number of clauses to negotiate in the contract, but it was almost sure that Ardith would be doing the picture. Josh's film was on a fast track and due to start shooting in March, and it would all be shot locally. Ardith's wouldn't start until May or June and would include a month of location shooting in Africa, and another month in England at the end of the film.

"What happens when you go on location?" Josh asked her. "I stay here and keep the home fires burning?"

"If you want to, or you can come with me if you've finished your movie by then." She smiled at him.

"I can come on location with you?" He was excited at the prospect. "That sounds like fun." Everything they were doing sounded like fun now.

"It is." She smiled at him again. "If we're lucky, our schedules will dovetail, or you can roam around exploring Africa while I'm working."

"Would I go as your assistant?" He wasn't sure of his role in her life yet, or how they were going to explain him.

"If you want to," she said easily. "Or you can come as you, an actor who just finished a movie and loves me." She looked happy and he was startled.

"You'd be okay with that?" he asked her.

"The truth is usually easier than a lie," she said. "Lies are a lot of work to maintain."

"I thought maybe you'd want to hide me for a while," he said shyly, and she laughed.

"You're hard to hide, Josh, and I don't want to be sneaking in and out of your tent on location in Africa. I might get eaten by a lion. I figure by then, if we're together, we'll be ready to own who we are in each other's lives and what we're doing. The only one we owe some kind of explanation to is Morgan, and she'll be pissed whatever we do. I'm not going to hide you, Josh. You deserve better than that. I'm not ashamed of you. I love you. And if you're crazy enough to want to be with an old bat like me, I might as well be proud of you and show off, until you come to your senses and leave me for a twenty-five-year-old."

"Don't count on it," he said, grinning, "that's never going to happen." She didn't believe him, but wished it were true.

"You never know," she said, trying to be philosophical about it. "You may be too busy shooting then, but I was thinking maybe we could make our debut at the Oscars, in March. It will cause some shock waves for a minute, and then someone else will do something outrageous and they'll forget about us."

"You'd go to the Oscars with me?" He looked stunned. "Red carpet and all that?"

"The whole enchilada," she said comfortably. "I told Joe Ricci about us, by the way. He was impressed." Josh was too, and very touched that she was willing to be seen with him publicly. She just wanted to give it a little more time out of respect for Bill West, but she wanted to be seen in public with Josh if they were in love and dating. She didn't want to live a lie with him, for either of their sakes. "Do you have a tux?" she asked him.

"Of course. Can we go on my Harley?" He grinned.

"No," she said, and laughed. "You're going to be a movie star one day, you can't go to the Oscars on a Harley. Besides, I'd probably fall on my ass in front of the theater on Hollywood Boulevard." He laughed at the image.

They went to one of their out-of-the-way restaurants that night for dinner and talked about the projects they had in store. Their horizons were expanding exponentially, and the future looked bright.

"I talked to Morgan today, by the way. She's going to Paris for a week. I think there's a man in her life, but she's not admitting it.

She's being very secretive, and I know when she's lying but didn't call her on it. Maybe he's married, or it's one of her partners. I hope whoever he is makes her happy. She's old enough to be with whoever she wants." Josh nodded and marveled at Ardith's ability for forgiveness, given how badly Morgan treated her. Ardith seemed to have a remarkable capacity to believe that things would turn out well in the end. He hoped she was right, and so far she had been, about them anyway. He still couldn't believe all the good things that had happened since he met her. She had a profound conviction that if you did things right, worked hard, were faithful, had integrity, and were an honest person, the right things would come, and it had been true so far. But he couldn't see Morgan changing any time soon. He was sure that she'd be a thorn in their side forever, while she punished her mother for past sins, both imagined and real. And unlike Ardith, Josh didn't believe that even the right man would change Morgan. Ardith was a profoundly good person, and Morgan was a bitch, as far as he was concerned, but he didn't say it to her mother. He hated the way Morgan treated her. Ardith deserved so much better. She was such a good woman, which her daughter didn't seem to appreciate.

When they got home that night, Ardith made him study his script, and quizzed him on some scenes he'd been working on with his drama coach. She was teaching him things he had never known, about acting, and the business, and he was always impressed by how talented she was, and how much he could learn from her.

After she had put him through his paces with the script, they climbed into her bed and made love. In Josh's opinion, their life was perfect, and there wasn't a single thing that he would have changed, least of all her age. He loved being in love with an adult who didn't play games. She was honest and outspoken and compassionate, and best of all, real. And she brought out the best in him. It was life without games.

When Ben and Morgan left for Paris, he had a heavy work schedule, and she had a long list of museum exhibits she wanted to see, but they had carved out time to spend together too. He wanted to take her to dinner at his favorite restaurants, both *gastronomique,* with Michelin stars, and simple bistros. He had taken a suite at the Ritz, mostly for her, and had justified it to the network because he was going to be conducting several interviews there with a French camera crew. And he was going to the Élysée Palace, the French White House, to interview the French president.

As soon as Morgan and Ben arrived at the Ritz, they got the full VIP treatment, and the suite was beautiful, with a view of the Place Vendôme. Morgan wanted to do some shopping too, as well as her list of museums and gallery shows. Paris was her favorite city. Ben had invited his daughter to dinner on their second night, at the Fontaine de Mars, the bistro he liked best.

It felt like a honeymoon as they settled into the hotel, got massages, and swam in the pool. They had room service that night, went to bed early, and made love in the luxurious bedroom of their suite.

They were both trying not to think of the trial by fire awaiting him in New York in the coming weeks, with the girl who claimed to be pregnant by him, the DNA test, and her threats of what she would tell the network if he didn't agree to pay her what she wanted as damages and support for her and a child. It was an enormous amount he could afford but wasn't looking forward to.

Neither of them brought up the subject, and Ben wanted the trip to Paris to strengthen his relationship with Morgan and give them the courage to face what lay ahead. But reality intruded when his assistant emailed him a mention on Page Six of the *Post* that a Tracy McCarthy, previously an intern on his show, was filing a paternity suit against him on behalf of herself and her unborn child. His assistant added that they'd already had dozens of calls about it. It was the hot news item of the hour and Tracy's first shot across their bow, to show that she meant business. There was no MeToo claim mentioned, just the paternity suit, which was enough for now. Ben showed it to Morgan, and sent an email to his assistant that she was to say he was on assignment out of the country and had no comment. And there had been no comments or questions from his bosses so far. They knew his reputation and weren't surprised. It wasn't a full-blown scandal yet, just gossip. And they'd know the truth in a couple of weeks, with the test Perry Blackstone would administer.

Ben had a full schedule the first day, with the interview with the president at the Élysée, and Morgan spent the day at the Louvre and the Jeu de Paume. She walked through the Tuileries Gardens and back to the hotel. She was dressed for dinner with Ben and his daughter when he got back to the hotel.

Morgan and Ben were meeting Amanda at eight. Amanda had decided not to bring her boyfriend since he didn't speak English and neither Morgan nor Ben spoke French. Ben had met him before and didn't like him. He was an artist and Ben said he looked a mess, and even in broken English managed to convey his extreme left political views, and his disapproval of people like them. Amanda had decided to spare her father a second round. Julien and her father were not destined to be friends. She had been living in Paris for four years, felt at home there, and was fluent in French.

Morgan didn't know what to expect when they left for the restaurant with a car and driver Ben had hired at the Ritz, and they headed for the Left Bank to the trendy but cozy bistro with excellent French food. Amanda was waiting for them outside the restaurant, smoking a cigarette. She had a wild mane of curly red hair, was slim and petite, and was wearing torn jeans, a paint-splattered T-shirt, combat boots, and a camouflage vest. She wasn't chic, or even tidy, and her hands were covered in paint too, but she looked lively and fun. She didn't look anything like her father, but she seemed pleased to see him, and she sized up Morgan as they walked into the restaurant together. They were about the same age and couldn't have been more different. Ben looked mildly uncomfortable as they sat down at the table, and Amanda pointed out that she hadn't seen him in nearly a year, which surprised Morgan.

Morgan asked Amanda about her life in Paris and told her about the exhibits she was planning to see, which impressed Amanda. She had seen several of them, and suggested some more obscure ones Morgan might enjoy, and a gallery that sold street art. She was fascinated by Morgan's medical career as a plastic surgeon. The two women got along better than Ben had hoped, and the three of them had a lively exchange about French politics. Ben described his interview with the French president that day, and Amanda made it clear that she agreed with Julien and that she was a supporter of the extreme left. It was an interesting evening, and Morgan had the feeling that Ben hardly knew his daughter, who was direct and outspoken and said that she had joined several protests. Ben looked uncomfortable when Amanda invited Morgan to lunch the next day at an artists' cafeteria near where she was taking classes. Morgan was intrigued by Amanda and accepted the invitation. She wanted to get to know her better, since Ben seemed to know so little about her.

When Ben kissed Amanda goodbye, she shot an acerbic comment at him. "See you next year, Dad," and he didn't comment. There was clearly some resentment there, and she wasn't shy about expressing it.

"I'm not thrilled at the idea of your having lunch with her tomorrow," he said to Morgan in the car on the way home.

"She's a bright woman, and I'd like to know more about her," Morgan said. She had enjoyed the evening, although normally the two women wouldn't have been friends, but they had her father in common. He didn't try to stop Morgan from going, but he was sorry she'd accepted the invitation.

"Her mother hates me, and she grew up hearing all that venom from her." Morgan wasn't surprised by it, and they went back to the grandeur of the Ritz, had a drink at the elegant Bar Vendôme, and then went to bed. It had been an enjoyable evening, and Morgan was happy she had come to Paris with Ben. She had sent her mother a text and told her where she was, but not the hotel. She knew her mother would guess instantly that she wasn't alone if she said she was staying at the Ritz. Morgan lived and traveled more modestly on her own.

Morgan met Amanda at the agreed-upon cafeteria the next day. It was a rough place full of scuzzy-looking people and artists. Amanda blended in perfectly, and Morgan had worn jeans and a down jacket and looked shockingly neat and clean compared to them. They stood on line for trays of food and sat down alone at a table as Amanda smiled at her.

"That was brave of you to agree to have lunch with me. Was my father pissed?"

Morgan smiled at the question. "Not pissed. Worried maybe," she said honestly. "Two women having lunch is usually bad news for any guy, especially if they're related to him." Amanda laughed at her answer.

"My parents hate each other. They got divorced when I was four, and I never saw him at all until I was about thirteen."

"Did you live somewhere else?"

"No, we lived in New York, in the Village. He just didn't want to see me. My mother finally shamed him into it. He was on the road most of the time then."

"It must have been hard for you not to see him," Morgan said sympathetically.

"I had a lot of illusions about him, and I think my mother wanted me to meet him so I'd agree with her that he's a jerk."

"And did you agree with her?" Morgan asked, curious.

"Not till later. He is kind of a jerk, but he's my father, and maybe it's better having a jerk as a father than none at all." It was an interesting point of view.

"My father died when I was seven. I had a lot of illusions about him too. He died in a helicopter crash with his girlfriend. My parents were still married, so mine was a jerk too. Maybe they all are," Morgan said, and Amanda laughed.

"My dad always brought some woman along whenever he saw me, the woman of the hour, and I don't think most of them lasted longer than that. You seem like something of an exception for him. They're usually twenty-two years old, twenty-five at most. You're ancient by his standards," she said jovially, and Morgan laughed.

"By mine too. He admits that he's had a lot of young women in his life. He claims he's reformed." She thought of Tracy McCarthy as she said it.

"I doubt that. Be careful," Amanda warned her. "'You can't teach an old dog new tricks.' You don't mind that he's so old?" Amanda asked her, and Morgan shook her head.

"I like it. Maybe he's the father I never had."

"Poor you," Amanda commented.

"He's more stable than younger men. Men don't play as many games at his age. Hopefully his wild and crazy days are behind him."

"I don't think they ever are for men like my father. He'll want a twenty-two-year-old when he's ninety, or in his grave. My mother says he cheated on her constantly. He probably did, thirty-five years ago. He was a sexy foreign correspondent, a star on TV, and a good-looking guy."

"He still is," Morgan commented.

"Then watch out for him. I wouldn't trust him if I were you. I'm sorry to say that if you love him, but my mom says a cheater is a cheater forever and I have found that to be true. Do you want kids?" She changed the subject abruptly and Morgan shook her head.

"No, I think I'm too old now. And I've never wanted them. I love my medical career. I work too hard to be a good mother. My mother was never around when I was a kid. She was always away, working. I don't want to do that to a child."

"What does she do?"

"She's an actress," Morgan said vaguely.

"So was mine, when my father met her. She quit when she had me, and never went back to work. Did yours stick with it?" Morgan nodded and debated about telling her the truth. She actually liked Amanda, even though they didn't have much in common, except Ben. But Amanda was honest and real.

"She did. She's still working. Ardith Law," Morgan said simply, and Amanda stared at her.

"Are you fucking shitting me? She's a huge deal. That must be so cool!" Amanda was shocked.

"Cool on the screen, yes, at home, not so cool. She was never there, she was always on location somewhere. She was never much of a mother."

"Neither was mine, and she didn't have fame as an excuse. She was always off with the boyfriend of the moment, and dumped me with my grandmother, or a friend or a babysitter." Morgan realized that they had more in common than they originally thought, absent fathers and inattentive mothers who were never around.

"Do you get along with her now?" Morgan inquired, and Amanda shrugged.

"Not really. More or less. She was a lousy mother when I was growing up. She's better now, as a friend, and it takes too much energy to stay pissed. I hated her all through my twenties and blamed her for everything, and when I turned thirty, I gave it up. She's who she is, and I'm who I am. All that stuff doesn't matter anymore. I'm not a kid now. At our age, we make our own lives and our own choices. I have a boyfriend I love, even if my parents don't like him. I don't need their permission to be me anymore." Amanda sounded healthy and well balanced, and Morgan envied her. She had as much reason to be angry as Morgan, maybe more so—her mother didn't sound like a winner and she only saw her father once a year—but she had moved on with her art and her life, her boyfriend and her politics, and what they thought of it didn't seem to matter to her. "Has your mother met my father?" Amanda asked her.

"Not yet. She doesn't know about him."

"Will she be upset because he's so much older?" Amanda was curious.

"Probably, he's a year older than my mother. My mother and I fight all the time," Morgan admitted.

"It's a waste of time. They're who they are, we won't change them. And we're who we are. I have lunch with my mother occasionally. She doesn't say much anymore. She knows I don't care what she thinks. Julien and I are thinking of having a baby. We're not going to get married, but it might be nice to have a kid. She'll probably have a fit over that, and so will my dad."

"He'll survive it if you do," Morgan said, and thought that he might be having a baby too, which would be much more shocking than Amanda having one out of wedlock, and his baby's mother was only

162

twenty-two years old. He was in no position to disapprove of his daughter, but probably would anyway. Listening to her put things into perspective for Morgan. All her life she had tried to change her mother and turn her into something she wasn't instead of accepting her as she was. And Ardith was much more accepting of Morgan now than Morgan was of her. As she thought about it, she could feel the anger seep out of her, like oil seeping out of an engine or air out of a tire. And Amanda was right, it took too much energy to stay angry, and there was no longer anything to be angry about, except the past, which it was too late to change.

They talked about Amanda's art for the rest of lunch. She loved living in Paris and living with Julien in a world of artists all around her. They had met in art school. He was a few years younger than Amanda and she said he was a good guy. "My father thinks he's a communist, but he's not, he's a socialist, and so am I. My dad and I don't have to agree on politics, or on anything really. All I have to do is have dinner with him once a year and meet the girl of the hour. I got lucky this time. I really enjoyed meeting you. I hope it works out for you and my dad, and he behaves. And if he doesn't, get rid of him, and find a guy who treats you right. I had a shit boyfriend before, but Julien is great." Amanda had such an easy, direct philosophy about life. She was like a breath of fresh air. Morgan wondered if Ben realized what a great daughter he had, and she suspected he didn't. But if he didn't, it was his loss more than his daughter's, who no longer expected anything from him except dinner once a year, which was hardly difficult to deliver.

They hugged outside the cafeteria, and Morgan walked back to the Right Bank. She felt freer and lighter when she did. Amanda had helped her ease her burdens. She was really happy to have met her, and she thought about her comments about Ben. They weren't reassuring, but they were honest and practical, particularly if things didn't work out. And her comments about her relationship with her mother had been helpful. There were definite parallels in their lives.

Morgan went to another museum that afternoon and was in good spirits when Ben came home from work and met her at the hotel.

"How did lunch go?" he asked, as he sipped the martini he had ordered.

"It was terrific. Amanda is amazing. She is a bottomless well of wisdom and sensible advice."

"She must have had plenty of bad stories about me, I assume," he said, not looking happy about it.

"No, more about her mother, who sounds like mine, or actually even less motherly. Amanda is amazingly open, philosophical, and forgiving. I may take some of her advice about my mother. I can't spend five minutes with her without fighting. Maybe it's time to give that up." Morgan knew she'd been tough on Ardith.

"Amanda's mother is a piece of work. I don't know how we lasted for more than a week," Ben said.

"You were both young, and you had Amanda to keep you together for a while, I guess. I think that was my parents' situation too. My father got caught when he died with his girlfriend. You were just luckier."

"Do you think she'll marry the communist?" he asked her, and she didn't want to give up Amanda's secrets about the baby they were planning without marriage.

"No, I don't think she'll marry him. They don't believe in mar-riage." Ben looked surprised at that.

"I just hope they don't have a baby out of wedlock," he added, and Morgan gave him a meaningful look.

"I hope *you* don't have a baby out of wedlock," she said, and he winced.

"You didn't tell her about that, did you?" He panicked.

"Of course not. I kept all your secrets. She's very accepting of you too. And she was very nice to me. She said she hopes it works out for us. So do I," Morgan added gently, to make up for her earlier com-ment.

"Me too," Ben agreed. They made love before they went out to dinner at Alain Ducasse, and they had a drink at the cozy famous Hemingway Bar at the Ritz that night when they got home. The trip to Paris was a big success so far, and gave them the time they needed together, with everything else going on in their lives. They both knew that all hell might break loose when they went home, but being in Paris was like being on another planet, where everything was beauti-ful, and nothing unpleasant could touch them. It was a perfect week in a magical place, and they were both sorry to leave and return to all the problems and demons waiting for them in New York. And for Morgan, meeting Amanda had been a very special gift.

Chapter 12

When Morgan and Ben got back to New York, they went to their own apartments. They had loved waking up together every day, but he had a heavy week ahead, and the French presidential interview to edit for a special on TV. Morgan had a heavy surgical schedule to make up for her time away.

Ben had a meeting with Stan Silver, his attorney, on the first day. Tracy McCarthy had an attorney of her own by then, and he was negotiating furiously on her behalf. He was trying to make a deal with Ben even before she had the DNA test, which made Stan highly suspicious of what the results would be. If the baby was Ben's, she wanted a lump sum and support for herself and the child until it reached the age of twenty-one. And if the baby wasn't his, she wanted a settlement of damages, with the threat that she would accuse him of rape and cost him his job if he didn't pay her. Either way, he was going to pay a shocking amount for having had sex with her. It was a high price to pay for a few hours of fun.

"It's very simple," Stan said to his client, "the woman is a flat-out crook. What she's doing is extortion. We can expose her and press charges, but I think we should get the results of the DNA test first, so we know what we're dealing with. If the child is yours, you're on the hook anyway, it just depends how much it will cost you. If the child isn't yours, she has a big gun in her hands in today's climate, if she accuses you of rape."

"She has no proof, and I didn't rape her," Ben said solemnly.

"I believe you, Ben," Stan said sympathetically, "but I can't promise you that a judge and jury will, or the head of the network. This is going to be embarrassing for them too. They may not care about a paternity suit that's quietly settled, but they will care a lot about the rape of a twenty-two-year-old intern who is going to give a great imitation of the Virgin Mary on the stand."

"I've never abused a woman in my life," Ben said, looking desperate, "and I didn't abuse her."

"No, but you've been indiscriminate about some of the women you slept with, and this is what you get for it. This girl is a two-bit crook, but she's smart and greedy. I have a feeling she set you up from the beginning, but we'll have a hell of a time proving it, and no one will believe us. As my grandmother used to say, 'You lie down with dogs, you get fleas.' And Tracy McCarthy is nobody's fool. Right now, she's winning, and she has some very heavy artillery aimed at you. You'll almost be better off if the baby is yours and you pay her a lump sum and child support for the next twenty-one years. Although the amounts they're suggesting are ridiculous. She's agreed to have the DNA test this week, but they want to make a deal first, *before* we even know if the baby is yours, which is highly suspicious. She wants to set up both scenarios before we get the results of the test. I think a judge would take a dim view of it, which is who would be hearing the case if we accuse her of extortion, but right now, it's all about money. That's what this whole case is about. She used her body to entrap you, and it worked. You walked right into her trap." Ben had never regretted having sex with a woman so much in his life, but it was too late now. The damage was done.

As soon as they got back, Morgan set up the DNA test with her friend Perry Blackstone. Tracy was eight weeks pregnant by now, the earliest it could be done. All they needed was a blood sample from Tracy, and either blood or saliva from Ben to conduct a fetal cell analysis. They would compare the fetal cells in Tracy's bloodstream to Ben's, and the results, seven working days later, would be ninety-nine percent accurate. It couldn't be simpler, and the results would be undeniable. In less than two weeks, Ben would know what he was in for. Paternity or the threat of an accusation of rape if the baby wasn't his. Either way he was on the hook and in grave danger. And if she accused him of rape, he would surely lose his job. Several men at the network had been fired in the last year for sexual misconduct.

Ben went back to work after his meeting with his attorney and felt sick for the rest of the day. Tracy was due to have her blood drawn the next morning. And he was due to have his own blood drawn the day after. His blissful week in Paris with Morgan felt as though it was years behind them.

Ben had to work late that night editing the French presidential piece, so Morgan didn't see him. She was surprised when Perry called her the next morning.

"It's a no-go," he said when Morgan came on the line between patients. "We couldn't do it."

"Why not?" She sounded surprised and wondered if Tracy had changed her mind and refused the test, which would be damning evidence against her and imply that she was lying, which would be good for Ben.

"This is just between us, as med school best friends. You know the HIPAA laws as well as I do, but I think you should know. So don't tell anyone. We did a routine exam and sono to make sure that she's eight weeks pregnant, since that's the earliest we can do the DNA test, and she must have confused her dates of LMP"—last menstrual period—"because she's not as pregnant as she said. She's a good two weeks shy of eight weeks, maybe ten days, but closer to two weeks. Date of conception is two weeks later than we were told," he said matter-of-factly. "Women get mixed up on their dates all the time, but my computers don't lie. We'd be wasting Ben Ryan's time and money if we did the blood draw now. We told her to come back in two weeks. We can get a totally reliable result then. It's not a big deal. It's only another two weeks to wait. She was pretty annoyed. She's a real piece of work. I don't know how he fell for that barracuda. She's nearly salivating at what she's going to get out of him. Not the kind of patient I enjoy. Pregnancy for profit. It makes you wonder what she'll do with the kid once she gets the money. She's using her reproductive organs as a goldmine."

Morgan felt sick as she listened, for a number of reasons, but the portrait he painted of Tracy wasn't a nice one, and Morgan knew from years of friendship that Perry was usually an easygoing guy. "I'll let you know when we get the result. If she's back for the blood draw in two weeks, and I'm sure she will be, you'll have the results, or he will, of the fetal cell analysis three weeks from now. I'm sure the wait seems interminable to Ryan, but in the scheme of things, it's not long to wait. Sorry we couldn't do it today. And I'll call you for that dinner you promised me after we get the result." He had to rush off to see a patient in labor then, and Morgan sat at her desk feeling as though she had been struck by lightning. What he had just told her, that Tracy was two weeks less pregnant than they'd thought, changed everything for Morgan. Since allegedly Ben had only had sex with her once, it could mean that he had had intercourse with her two weeks later than he said, *after* he had met Morgan and was wooing her, *not before*. While he was wining and dining Morgan and telling her that she was The One and that he had never felt that way before, sometime between his dinners with Morgan and their initial kisses, and maybe even after he had made love to her, he could have had sex with Tracy, which would make him a liar and a cheater, and not the innocent victim he was pretending to be. But the joke was on him, if you could call it that, since Tracy had gotten pregnant. *Or* he had had sex with Tracy when he said he did, and she had gotten pregnant by someone else two weeks later. So, either she was the most dishonest woman on the planet and framed Ben with the full intent of extorting money from him or, if the baby was his, he had slept with her two weeks later than he said and cheated on Morgan. But a doubt had been cast, and no one knew the truth now. Morgan sat in her office tormenting herself about it, and called Perry back minutes later. He came to the phone and sounded rushed.

"I'm sorry to bug you," she said apologetically.

"No worries, I've got a primigravida in early labor and I just sent her to the hospital. She's got hours to go. What's up?"

"I'm just wondering about those computers of yours. Did they give you a date of conception? They must have if you know she was two weeks shy of eight weeks."

"Yeah, they give us a date, and they're pretty accurate. Let me check, give me a second." He put her on hold for a minute and then came back on the line. He gave her the date and she jotted it down.

"That's terrific, thanks, Perry," she said.

"No problem. Talk to you soon. And remember, don't let on that you know." He hung up, and she sat staring at the date she had written down. She flipped through her appointment book, but she already knew the answer. Tracy had gotten pregnant after Morgan had spent the weekend with Ben, passionately making love. Tracy had gotten pregnant the week of Bill's funeral, when Ben hadn't called or seen Morgan for five days, had stood her up for dinner and disappeared. He was having sex with Tracy then, maybe even more than once. Morgan felt sick as she stared at her datebook, and folded the slip of paper with the fateful date into it. If the baby was his, it had happened after he and Morgan met. Morgan no longer believed him when he said he had sex with Tracy right before he met Morgan. The doubt in Morgan's mind was great now. He had cut it too close, and she just didn't believe him. As Amanda's mother had told her, once a cheater, always a cheater. And more than likely, Ben was.

Ben called her late that afternoon, sounding discouraged.

"Did you hear what happened?" he asked her. "We have to wait another two weeks for the test, which means another seven to ten days for the results after that. Maybe she got pregnant by someone

171

else after she slept with me. Anything is possible with a girl like that," and possibly a man like him.

"I'm sorry you have to wait." She didn't tell Ben that she had the date of conception now, and that it had happened after she went to L.A. She didn't want to get in an argument with him about when he had sex with Tracy, and when he didn't, and if it was before or after he had slept with Morgan. It was all too hazy now, and there were too many possibilities and unanswered questions. She wasn't sure if she would ever feel the same way about him and trust him again. She doubted it. It was all too vague, and the timing was very close. She couldn't be sure when Ben had slept with Tracy. But if Tracy was pregnant by Ben, it had happened after he and Morgan had started dating.

"Are you coming over tonight?" he asked her. He liked waking up next to her, as they had in Paris. But it was a lot to ask now, with the specter of Tracy McCarthy between them, and so much uncertainty about what had really happened.

"I have an awful headache," she said as an excuse. "I think I may stay home tonight. It's probably jetlag."

"And stress," he said, feeling guilty. "I'm sorry to put you through this with me." He sounded sincere, but it was hard to know what to believe.

"It's worse for you," she said, trying to be compassionate about it, but she was angry at him, furious in fact, and she didn't trust him, which was worse.

"I can take care of you, if you want to come over," he said gently. And if she didn't? Who would he have sex with that night? She could no longer get the image of Tracy out of her head. "Tomorrow then," he said. "Maybe we should go away somewhere this weekend. It might do us good. It's going to be a long three or four weeks now, waiting for the test and the results." The longest of her life, and even once they had the results, she would never know exactly for sure when he had slept with Tracy, or if he had been cheating on Morgan when he did. Maybe once a cheater, always a cheater was the rule he lived by. If so, he hadn't changed.

She didn't answer her phone that night when Ben called her, she pretended to be asleep. She hesitated again when her mother called her, and reluctantly picked it up. Her mother sounded cheerful and relaxed.

"Welcome home. How was Paris? Was it fun?"

"It was wonderful, it always is." Morgan tried to sound enthused about it, but she couldn't pull it off. She was too upset about Ben.

"Are you okay? You sound upset." Her mother was worried. Ardith knew her only child well, even if they didn't get along. They had thirty-eight years of experience with each other. It counted for something.

"Everything's kind of a mess at the moment," Morgan said vaguely.

"At work?"

"No, in my life." She hesitated for a moment while Ardith waited. She didn't want to rush Morgan. It was only six o'clock in California, and Josh was at the gym. Morgan finally spoke again. "I've been seeing someone for a couple of months. I didn't say anything because I didn't know if it would turn into something important or not. And it kind of slipped off the rails pretty quickly. He's an unusual person."

"Do you love him?" Ardith went straight to the heart of the matter.

"Yes, sort of . . . maybe . . . I don't know. It's very confusing at the moment. He's in a difficult situation and I don't know what to believe."

Ardith could hear how upset and confused Morgan was. "Do I know him?" Morgan waited a long beat before she answered.

"The whole world knows him. Ben Ryan." She heard her mother gasp.

"Good Lord. Yes, I know who he is. He's older than I am, isn't he?" Ardith was trying not to be shocked.

"Only by a year."

"Is he married?"

"No, he's single, divorced twice. He has a daughter more or less my age. I just met her in Paris. I liked her. Anyway, to cut to the chase, I fell for him like a ton of bricks, as they say. It's been going on for about two months. Sometimes it's wonderful, and sometimes it isn't. And he stupidly slept with someone else around the time he met me. Now she's pregnant and trying to slap him with a paternity suit. And if it turns out the baby isn't his, when they have a DNA test, then she's threatening him with a MeToo suit. She's trying to extort money from him however she can get it, and he could lose his job. So that's about it, and my dilemma is that I can't figure out if he slept with her before he met me or after. The timing is very close."

"What does he say?"

"Before. But I'm not sure I believe him. Other than that, everything's great," Morgan said cynically. "It must sound crazy to you. It does to me."

"The girl sounds like a complete criminal, for one thing. Ben Ryan must be a mess at the moment. He's got a lot on the line."

"He does. I don't know why I'm telling you all this now. There's nothing you can do about it."

"I can listen. It's a lot to be carrying alone."

"Yes, it is," Morgan agreed. She was impressed that her mother hadn't said anything critical about how much older Ben was, or the fact that he had slept with a slut who was trying to extort money from him. It was hardly testimony to the kind of women he went out with. All Ardith sounded was sad for Morgan, and sympathetic to Ben. Morgan would never have believed it.

"Has she agreed to the DNA test?"

"Yes, but she wants to make a deal for the money before the results."

"She sounds like a real con artist. Every man's nightmare."

"He was an idiot to sleep with her, and without protection. He realizes that now, but he's old enough to know better."

"People do stupid things at times," Ardith said kindly. "What's the real problem for you? The baby?"

"No, he doesn't want the baby or the girl. It's that I don't know if I can trust him. I don't think I believe him about when he slept with her. It might have been after I came out for Bill's funeral. But if the baby's not his, then he might be telling the truth, and it was right before me, and she got pregnant by someone else after he slept with her. It's all up in the air right now and kind of a blur."

"Do you want to come home for a few days and chill out?" Ardith asked her without judgment or comment.

"I can't, Mom, I have to work. I just took a week off for Paris. And everyone in New York wants work done on their face this time of year, after the holidays. We've been backed up around the block for two months."

"How did you meet him, by the way?" her mother asked her.

"He was a patient," Morgan said glumly.

"He had a face-lift?" Ardith seemed shocked, although many male actors she worked with had them.

"No, he was in a bombing in India and got a scar on his cheek that my senior partner worked on. They went to Harvard together."

"Well, you didn't pick a dumb one. He's a very interesting man. I've always liked him on TV and his specials are excellent."

"Yes, he is interesting. I was crazy about him, now I don't know if I can trust him, ever again."

"What does your gut tell you?" Ardith asked her seriously.

"I know that he's always been a cheater. He says he's changed. Or is it once a cheater, always a cheater? That's what his ex-wife says about him."

"You met her too?" Ardith was surprised.

"No, his daughter told me. She's smart too. She's an artist in Paris. I had lunch with her, and dinner. She says he was a lousy father, but she likes him anyway. She's kind of a character."

"Do you really want to be with a man in his sixties? Twenty years from now he'll be a very old man, and you'll still be young, and a nurse."

"I wouldn't care if he was in his nineties, if he's the right one. I thought he was. Now I'm not sure."

"Why don't you wait and see what the DNA test says?"

"That's not the crux of it for me. What matters to me is *when* he slept with her, before or after he started with me, and if he's telling me the truth. A liar would be as bad as a cheater."

"He doesn't have much to lie about at this point. He's pretty heavily exposed." And then Ardith's voice softened. "Thank you for telling me, Morgan. I wish I could be more help." She was touched that Morgan had told her. Ardith always wished that they could be closer, but Morgan rarely allowed it and kept her at a distance. Morgan had rarely been forgiving, even as a child, and could hold a grudge forever. And she had never forgiven her mother's mistakes and failings when Morgan was a child.

"I guess I'll know eventually what I want to do. It's going to be a long few weeks waiting for the results. A friend of mine from med school is doing the test. He isn't supposed to tell me the results, but I know he will, as a friend."

"I'd like to meet Ben sometime, if you stay with him," Ardith said gently.

"If I do, you will. This is some introduction. Thank you for being nice about it, Mom. It's not a pretty story."

"No, but these things happen. It's real life. And who knows what I'd have done if your father had survived the accident. Maybe I'd have taken him back. I was madly in love with him. It was easier hating him after he died, instead of mourning him. I still loved him. Your father got caught by circumstances. Ben got caught by a greedy woman. Maybe the two aren't so different. People are weak sometimes. They're human. Do you think he'll pay her off to save his job?"

"Probably. He could get fired anyway. Sex scandals aren't tolerated these days. It sounds like she set him up, if what he says is true. And I believe him."

"I have faith that you'll make the right decision," Ardith said with certainty and faith in her daughter. Morgan was a smart woman.

"I hope so. I'd rather meet the right guy at forty than hang on to the wrong one at thirty-eight. Right now, I don't know which one he is."

"You'll figure it out."

"Thanks, Mom." Some part of her conversation with Amanda had found its way to Morgan's soul. She wasn't angry at her mother anymore. It was the first time in years she had talked to her mother as a friend, and Ardith hadn't disappointed her. She had listened and refrained from any criticism. She just wanted the best for Morgan, and neither of them knew what that was. And for Ardith, loving Josh had shown her that age really didn't matter, except to the people involved. It was up to them, and up to Morgan in this case if she wanted to put up with Ben's mess and stick by him. No one else could decide it for her. Ardith worried about her, but she recognized that Morgan was old enough to make her own decisions, and she trusted her to make the right ones.

Morgan felt better when they hung up, and she sent Ben a text before she went to bed. "I love you. See you tomorrow?" He was awake and answered immediately, relieved to hear from her. It had been a hard day for both of them.

"Yes! And I'm so sorry," was his response.

"I know. So am I," she sent back to him, smiling sadly, and went to bed, wondering if they'd survive it. But at least her mother had been nice. And she knew about Ben now.

"What was that about?" Josh asked her. He'd heard the last half of the conversation at Ardith's end when he got back from the gym. She told him about Ben's situation, and he looked serious as he listened.

"That's every man's worst nightmare."

"He could lose his job if she accuses him of rape to extort money from him."

"Isn't he about sixty-five years old?" Josh asked her.

"Something like that, sixty-three, I think."

"Isn't that too old for Morgan?" He looked concerned.

"We're in no position to make comments about that," Ardith reminded him, and he laughed.

"I guess you're right. Did you tell her about us?"

"No, she's got enough on her plate without dealing with us on top of it. There's time to tell her. And she'll see us at the Oscars."

"Will she have a fit?"

"I doubt it now. I think what she's going through with Ben Ryan will open her eyes to what matters. It sounds like it already has. She was very open with me, which doesn't happen often."

"He seems like a pretty cool guy, other than his sex scandal. Wouldn't you rather be with someone like him?" he asked her shyly, and she turned to him and kissed him.

"Just shut up, and no I would not want to be with him. I want to be with you."

"Good. Because I'm not going anywhere. I hope he gets his mess sorted out, though. It sounds bad."

Ardith thought about it all evening, and the dilemma Morgan was facing. She wasn't sure what she'd have done herself in the same situation, and hoped she'd never have to face it. She admired her daughter for trying to be fair to Ben, and true to herself, and hoped she came to the right conclusion, whatever it was. She'd have to figure out if he was a liar or a cheater, or a good guy who had made a terrible mistake. For now, there was no way to know.

Chapter 13

T he night after she spoke to her mother, Morgan spent the night
with Ben. They had a quiet evening at home, cooked dinner
together, and avoided the subject of the postponed DNA test that was
hanging over their heads. There was no point talking about it until
they knew the results. Morgan spent the weekend with Ben, then
alternated between nights with him and nights alone. She needed
time to herself to think about things. Ben didn't press her about it.

And Ben's attorney continued to negotiate with Tracy's. They had
come to a tentative agreement by the time she took the test two
weeks later. Ben's blood had already been drawn, and after Tracy
was tested, they had ten more days to wait for the results.

The agreement Ben had tentatively consented to was more than
generous. If the baby was his, Tracy wanted five hundred thousand
dollars, and Stan had negotiated her down to two hundred thousand, with ten thousand a month for her and the child for twenty-
one years. Ben would pay for all schools and college and provide

medical insurance for both Tracy and the child. He could afford it, but it was an enormous amount for a woman he had only met once and had casual sex with. Visitation was to be negotiated in the coming months. He hadn't decided yet if he wanted to see the child or not. He was bitter about what she had done.

If the baby wasn't his, she wanted five hundred thousand dollars in damages, nonnegotiable, not to accuse him of rape. She had wanted a million, but Stan Silver had refused it out of hand. Half a million was more than enough. And Ben still wanted to prosecute her for extortion. She wanted a signed agreement that he wouldn't, which he was refusing to sign. It was a bitter battle.

The day after her blood draw for the fetal cell analysis, another mention appeared on Page Six of an alleged paternity suit being brought by Tracy McCarthy. Ben's stomach turned over when he saw it. He was afraid it would go viral on the internet. He was staring at the *Post* in despair as he sat at his desk, when his assistant told him there was a Betsey Lane on the phone who insisted she had to talk to him on an urgent personal matter.

"Shit," he muttered to himself, debating whether to speak to her or not. He was afraid she was a reporter, or someone else wanting to extort money from him. In the end, he picked it up. He was in so deep already, it couldn't make much difference. "Yes?" he barked into the phone, and the woman at the other end sounded nervous when she answered.

"I have documents that will help you," she said in barely more than a whisper.

"Who is this? What kind of documents?" He was instantly tense.

"My name is Betsey Lane. I work for the Lewison Sperm Bank. I have a file of a purchase made two months ago that I think will be important for you. No one can know if I give them to you. I could lose my job." She was offering to violate the HIPAA laws of privacy, which was a very serious offense, but she had read the item on Page Six, and she had guessed that Tracy McCarthy was trying to ruin Ben's life, probably to extort money from him, which Betsey thought was disgusting if she was right, and she wanted to help him.

"I'm about to lose mine. And just how much do you want to sell them to me for? A million? Two million?" He was angry. He felt like a dog that had been kicked once too often, and he was ready to bite anyone now. The stress of the last month had gotten to him severely. He had lost weight and had dark circles under his eyes. He looked ill.

"I don't want anything," she said. "I think someone is accusing you falsely of paternity. These files may help you defend yourself." Something about what the woman was saying rang true to him. She didn't sound like a con artist. The DNA test would solve the paternity, but he was curious about what files the woman was referring to.

"When can I see them? Where can I meet you?" The woman mentioned a delicatessen downtown on the West Side. It sounded like a wild-goose chase, but he was willing to try anything. If she was telling the truth, whatever she had might turn the tides that were about to drown him. His relationship with Morgan was at the breaking point. His nerves were raw. He was sure that his superiors at the network were aware of at least some of what was going on, with two mentions of a paternity suit on Page Six of the *Post*. "How soon can you get there?" Ben asked her.

"I have a break in half an hour. It's a ten-minute walk from my office. The files are already in my purse. I was going to drop them off

183

at your office. I made copies, but I have the originals, you might need them to go to the police." She sounded serious, and he felt like he was in a movie.

"You're either a saint or this is another scam, and if it is I swear I'm going to beat you to a pulp whoever you are." He couldn't take much more of this, and he felt as though he had aged ten years in a month and looked it. And Morgan was looking worn out too. Her mother had been texting her messages of support but didn't want to annoy her and call her. Ardith knew that Morgan would call if she needed her and wanted to talk, and she hadn't. But their one conversation had helped calm Morgan for now.

Ben put his coat on and left his office as soon as he hung up, and muttered to his assistant on the way out that he'd be back in a couple of hours, with no further explanation. He had forgotten to ask for a description of the woman who had called him, and he had no idea who she was and what she looked like. He would just have to figure it out when he got there.

It took him half an hour to get downtown from his office. Traffic was heavy, but he was right on time when he saw the deli. He walked in, and it was half empty—the morning customers were gone except for a few tables of old people from a retirement center nearby, and it was too early for the lunch crowd. He was looking around trying to figure out who Betsey Lane was, when a heavyset middle-aged woman walked in, looking nervous. She was carrying a large purse and saw him immediately. He walked over to her, and he could tell that she recognized him.

"Ms. Lane?" he asked her in a low voice, and she nodded, afraid that someone would hear them. She had never done anything like this before. She was scared but looked determined. "Thank you for coming," he said kindly, trying to make up for his outburst on the phone, threatening to beat her to a pulp. He wasn't a violent person, but Tracy McCarthy had driven him to the edge of what he could tolerate.

He pointed to a nearby table and they sat down. A waiter came over and they ordered two cups of coffee. He set them down a minute later and Betsey Lane wrestled a large manila envelope out of her purse and handed it to Ben. He took out the contents. It was a file marked confidential, and in it was a photograph of Tracy McCarthy, the intern who was trying to destroy his life. There were two photographs of unidentified men, and computer simulations of what their children would look like, if Tracy used their sperm to become pregnant. They were ordinary-looking young men who looked like college students, with brown hair and brown eyes like his. The notes said that one went to Columbia, the other to NYU, and both were medical students. It said that one was twenty-one and the other twenty-two. There were health histories for both of them. Betsey Lane directed him to two other sheets of paper further into the file.

"She made withdrawals on two separate days." Ben saw immediately that one withdrawal from the bank was ten days after he had sex with her, and the second withdrawal was the day after that. He'd had sex with her a few nights before he met Morgan at her office to check his scar. And Tracy had purchased the sperm ten and eleven days later, in case she hadn't gotten pregnant by him. So, for now, before the DNA test, she probably didn't know who the father of her unborn baby was, but she had wanted to get pregnant, and she must have figured that she had sex with Ben too early and decided to make sure she got pregnant by using the donor sperm. There was one chance in three that the baby was his, depending on when she ovulated, but she had covered herself financially with the extortion scam she'd come up with, threatening to charge him with rape. Ben looked up at his benefactor in surprise.

"Why are you giving me this?" He knew full well the seriousness of the HIPAA violation, and Betsey Lane had no reason to help him except that she was a decent human being, and Tracy's name had rung a bell when she read it and could guess her motive.

"When I saw the mention of the paternity suit on Page Six, I realized that she was probably trying to get money from you. But she bought the sperm to get pregnant. I guess she was going to try to fool you that the fetus was yours. I think she's lying to you. I can't give you the donors' names, but the withdrawal slips tell enough," Betsey Lane said with a serious expression. She didn't want to impact the donors' lives too, only to help Ben. "I've been watching you on TV for years and you look like a nice man. We don't run the sperm bank to try and fool people, or help people blackmail someone for money. Is that what she's doing?" Ben nodded. It was one of those unforgettable moments in life when something crazy happens that changes everything. It was a miracle that Betsey had come forward, and he was sure it would help in some way, and it showed Tracy McCarthy's intent to get pregnant and extort money from him. She had done everything humanly possible to get pregnant, and then pin it on him. She probably hadn't expected the DNA test, although she should have, going after someone like him, but the rape threats and the signed agreement she wanted not to prosecute told the rest of the story. Her lawyer was as dishonest as she was, hired on a contingency basis. He would take a percentage up front of whatever she got from Ben.

"I can't thank you enough," Ben said to Betsey Lane, with tears in his eyes. It was the kindest thing anyone had ever done for him, and she was a total stranger with a good heart. She could have said nothing, and she had decided that in this instance, the HIPAA laws weren't protecting Tracy, they were allowing her to injure another human being for financial gain. It was a violation of their intent.

"I made a copy of the file for the center. I'm giving you the originals. I think you'll need them." He nodded, he thought so too. "Will you go to the police with them?"

"Probably. I'm going to show them to my lawyer right away."

"I hope you can stop her before she can cause you any more trouble," the woman said. "When I saw the two mentions in Page Six, it clicked and I guessed what she was doing. I couldn't let that happen. No one deserves that. A baby isn't a weapon."

"I agree. This should help a lot." He looked at her gratefully.

"Does she want a lot of money?"

"Yes, she does. She wanted half a million dollars if the baby is mine, and a million dollars not to accuse me of rape if it isn't. One way or another, she's after a lot of money."

"She should be in jail," Betsey Lane said, and Ben felt suddenly guilty toward his benefactor. She had been brave to take the files and come forward to give them to him.

"I know on the phone I said . . . but would you like something for these files?" She had put her job on the line to help a total stranger.

"No, no, I just wanted to help you." She looked shocked at the implication of money. In her eyes, it would have made her as bad as Tracy. She didn't want a penny for helping him. She just wanted to do what was right, even if it meant breaking rules that she'd always respected.

"You've helped me incredibly. Would you like something to eat? A sandwich, a piece of pie?"

"No, thank you. I should get back. Call me if I can do anything else."

"What you've done is amazing." He put it all back in the manila envelope. What she had done was like a miracle fallen from the sky. They both stood up, and he left money on the table for the coffee and a tip and followed her out of the deli. He joined her on the sidewalk, thanked her again, hailed a cab, and got in, clutching the envelope to his chest as he rode uptown to Stan Silver's office. Ben told the receptionist it was urgent, and Stan came out three minutes later.

"What's up? It's too early for results," he reminded Ben.

"I have something to show you." Ben followed Stan into his office, took the file out of the envelope, and put it on Stan's desk. Stan looked through it without comment, stopping at the pertinent pages, and the two receipts for what Tracy had paid for the sperm. She'd made a nine-hundred-dollar investment for the two withdrawals, to ruin Ben's life, and set herself up financially with anywhere up to a million dollars, or twenty-one years of support dishonestly obtained.

"What a clever little bitch," Stan said in amazement as he looked at Ben.

"What do we do now?" Ben asked him.

"I take this to the district attorney and we bring charges for extor-tion, and fuck her agreement. If the kid is yours, you'll have to support it. If it isn't, you're off the hook, and with proof like this, I think her rape charges just went up in smoke."

"What do you think she'll do?" Ben asked him, slumped in a chair. He didn't look like his usual impeccable self. He looked disheveled and stressed, but he was smiling.

"If you didn't get her pregnant, I think she'll get an abortion, and she may go to jail, where she belongs. I have a friend in the DA's office, I want to see him right away. All we need now are the test results in about a week, and if it's not your kid, you'll have your life back and keep your job. With proof like this of what she tried to do, I don't think she'll pursue the rape charge, with no evidence to support it."

"I could take a lie detector test, if they want one."

"I doubt they will," Stan said.

Stan walked him out, and Ben called Morgan from the cab on the way back to his own office and told her what had happened. Out of the blue, an angel had fallen from the sky in the form of Betsey Lane, who wanted to see justice served. She was just a decent human being who had had the courage to reach out to him and had saved him, and his job.

Morgan was as relieved as he was. They still didn't know if he had fathered a baby, but things were looking up. And for the first time since Ben had told her the story, Morgan believed him. All they had to hope now was that the baby wasn't his. If it was, he had lied about the date of conception, and he had cheated on Morgan. If it wasn't, he had told her the truth.

* * *

Stan called Ben that afternoon. His friend in the DA's office wanted to wait until they had the DNA results to make it a stronger case against Tracy. And they only had another week to wait for the results, ten days at most.

It felt like an eternity as they waited, but Morgan stayed with him. He could tell that she was more confident about him and that she loved him.

"Do you believe me now that it happened right before I met you?" The sperm bank files supported his story and the timing. It was easier to believe him now, and she nodded.

"I don't want to worry in future about who you're having sex with if I'm not around."

"Morgan, I swear I won't do something like that to you. It was before you. Not by much. But I knew the moment I laid eyes on you that you were the woman I've looked for all my life. It happened with her a few days before I met you. I was an idiot. It wasn't planned, or a date. She offered herself up to me in a way she guessed correctly I wouldn't refuse. She was hot and young, and I hadn't met you yet. I was bored. It's sometimes hard to turn down an opportunity like that. I don't think a lot of single guys would have turned her down, or even married ones." He was being honest with her and she could sense it now. "I was a complete fool, and I paid a hell of a price for it, or almost did. But I learned a powerful lesson. My days of random meaningless casual sex are over. That girl had trouble written all over her, and I ignored it."

Morgan wanted to believe that his cheating days were over too. It wasn't cheating with Tracy, since he didn't have a relationship with anyone, but it was an extremely foolhardy thing to do. Tracy had picked him out to set him up. And he had fallen for it. In addition, he was famous and a prime target for opportunists and criminals. He couldn't afford to be careless, and he had been, insanely so.

"Can you forgive me?" he asked her, pleading with her.

"Yes, I can, but I have to be able to trust you," she said honestly. "I'm worried that you haven't seen the last of this girl yet. I can feel it. She's gone too far out on a limb to trap you, to give up this easily. She can still accuse you of rape, although she'll be a lot less credible now."

"When she gets arrested for extortion, that will be a strong message to her," Ben said grimly.

"If it's your baby, she has the winning card."

"Let's hope she doesn't," he said, grateful that Morgan hadn't left him. The results of the DNA test were crucial now.

Perry Blackstone called Ben first when the test results came in a day earlier than expected. He thought it was the right thing to do, to put him out of his misery quickly.

Ben took his call immediately.

"The baby's not yours. You're a free man, once you get the rape accusation dropped," Perry told him, and Ben closed his eyes with relief as he sat at his desk. "Congratulations!" Ben called Stan Silver then with the good news. And then he called Morgan and told her, while Stan called the district attorney. Ben hadn't signed the papers, and Tracy had already taken the test so she couldn't change her story. When Perry called Tracy to tell her the results after he called Ben, she said that Ben hadn't heard the last of it, and he was a liar and a cheat. He hadn't signed the agreement, and she said she could still accuse him of rape, and intended to.

Tracy had no idea that Stan had gone to the DA, or that they had the file from the sperm bank.

Three days later, two police officers showed up at the office where she was working as a temp, arrested her with a warrant, and took her out in handcuffs. They took her to jail, where she was booked for extortion and fraud. She was pregnant from the sperm she'd purchased. The police had the sperm bank file as evidence. Her plan had gone awry. And Ben was free. Completely free of all accusations and charges, and he had told the truth about the timing.

Tracy spent the night in jail and was arraigned the next day. She pleaded not guilty to both charges, and a friend paid her bail. Trial was set for six months later since it wasn't a violent crime, and there were worse cases on the books. She was liable to go to jail for six months or a year for fraud and an additional year for second-degree coercion, or even get probation since it was a first offense, but it was a powerful lesson to her. She had seen Ben as an easy target, and knew of his reputation as a womanizer, but he was a lot smarter than she thought. And Betsey Lane had tipped the scale for him.

Morgan called her mother that afternoon and told her, and Ardith was enormously relieved for both of them.

"How do you feel about him now?" Ardith asked her.

"I love him. I need to let the good news sink in. I need to know that I can trust him. I don't want him sleeping with every girl who throws herself at him. But I believe him now that it happened before me."

"That trust may take time," Ardith said gently. "You two need some time now without a crisis or a drama. You've been through a lot together. And I'm sure he learned a lesson from this." Ardith was smiling when she hung up and told Josh the good news.

"He's one lucky guy. He could have been screwed. She could have gotten pregnant by him, and he could have lost his job if she accused him of rape. She sounds like a lunatic, and a real piece of work. And in his position, he's at high risk."

Ardith agreed with him. "I hope that girl leaves him alone now. He and Morgan need some time together with none of this drama going on. It's been hard on both of them."

"Thank God the baby isn't his," Josh said again, grateful that nothing like it had ever happened to him. He had taken some chances too when he was younger, but he had no money for anyone to get. Ben was a big target and had taken a high risk.

Josh and Ardith took a long walk on the beach that afternoon. Josh was ready to start his movie soon, and Ardith was preparing for hers in June. Their lives were moving forward at a rapid pace.

In New York, Morgan spent the night with Ben, and for the first time in weeks, they both slept like babies, and as she looked at Ben, she wished that she could wind the film of their life back to the beginning when they met, and start over. But this wasn't a movie, it was real life, where you couldn't go back, only forward. She was thinking about that when she fell asleep, and about how lucky they were that Tracy's baby wasn't his.

Chapter 14

The hairdresser and manicurist had just left. Ardith preferred doing her makeup herself. And her dress was hanging from a hook in her dressing room. She had borrowed it from Chanel in Beverly Hills. It was a gold lace gown, which molded her figure like a second skin. The time she'd been spending with a new trainer was paying off. She was wearing nude lace underwear and high-heeled gold sandals when Josh walked in.

"I love your outfit. Won't you be cold?" he asked her with a grin. Benicia helped Ardith put the dress on, and she looked like a goddess when she did. Her hair was in a loose bun, and she was wearing a borrowed gold and diamond necklace. "You look spectacular," he said, admiring her as she turned slowly on one heel for him.

"You're pretty fabulous yourself. The tux really suits you," she said, and kissed him. It was going to be their first big public outing together, and she could see that Josh was nervous.

He had just started filming his first big movie and it was going well so far. He was well prepared, and the director had been helping him with additional guidance. Josh was applying himself diligently and wanted to make Ardith proud of him and justify her faith in him. She had visited him on the set, but didn't want to make him nervous, so she didn't go too often. But what she had seen so far impressed her. He was going to be a fine actor, and everyone thought the film was going to be a box office success. She was starting her own movie in three months, in June.

They were going to the Academy Awards that night, which she had warned him could be boring, but he was thrilled to be with her for such an important event.

They left the house at five o'clock to be on the red carpet at the Dolby Theatre by five-thirty. She had briefed him on what would happen and when, and warned him that when the full media corps pressed forward it could be overwhelming. He said he was ready for it.

She smiled at him as they sat in the limousine. She had a shimmering golden stole to go with the dress, and when they reached the Dolby Theatre on Hollywood Boulevard, Ardith stepped out and the crowd went crazy, shouting her name. She looked even better than she usually did, and she had a new look. Younger and fresher, and sexier. She was no longer part of an older couple of Hollywood legends. She was an icon herself, on the arm of a handsome young man who looked at her adoringly.

"What's his name?" the reporters shouted at her.

"Josh Gray!" she called back, and they shot dozens of photos of the couple as they advanced into the hotel lobby toward the red carpet.

"Wow, that's intense," Josh whispered to her. "They love you."

"Pretty soon they'll all know your name and they'll love you too."

"Do I walk behind you?" he whispered to her, and she tucked her hand into his arm.

"You walk with me. Just smile a lot. You look gorgeous," she complimented him, and was proud to be with him.

"So do you," he returned the compliment, as they made their way down the red carpet like royalty, posing for photographs, as TV reporters stuck their microphones at her and asked her who she thought would win.

"Who's your handsome escort?" several of them asked her.

"Josh Gray," she said proudly, and the reporters saw something in her eyes that hadn't been there before, and suddenly they caught on and started passing the word.

"Give us another shot . . . another smile . . . kiss her . . ." By the time Ardith and Josh reached the auditorium, the photographers had figured out that they were a couple and intensified their focus on them.

"You two look great together," one of them shouted at the couple.

"They think I'm your grandmother," Ardith whispered to Josh, and he shook his head with a rueful look.

"My grandmother never looked like that! She looked like the witch in 'Hansel and Gretel.' Thank you for bringing me," he whispered as they bantered. Ardith looked totally relaxed, and Josh was trying to look sophisticated and smooth and doing a good job of it. They stopped dozens of times to greet people and Ardith introduced him to everyone. When they finally took their seats in the enormous auditorium, she had seen everyone she wanted to, and everyone had seen them. It reminded her of all the times she had been there with

Bill in twelve years, and she missed him, like an old friend, or a brother. It was all different with Josh. He was young and vital and alive, he exuded sex appeal, he put an arm around her and kissed her, and Ardith smiled.

"That will be all over the press tomorrow," she told him. "We're big news." It was exciting to be with him and made the evening more fun for her. And Josh couldn't believe he was standing with every major star in Hollywood, and that he was Ardith Law's escort.

"This is so unreal," he whispered to her after they sat down. He recognized every single famous actor and actress within fifty feet of them.

"It's part of your reality now, not all of it, but an important part." The Academy Awards were a major Hollywood event, the biggest of the year, she reminded him. He was well aware of it, and grateful to be there, and for everything she'd done for him—his agent, her advice, the drama coach who had already taught him so much, all the doors she was opening for him, because she believed in him and loved him. The difference in their ages may not have made sense, but everything else did, and Josh had been the one to tell her that love didn't always make sense, and maybe it didn't have to.

He was impressed too by how hard Ardith worked. She'd been studying the script for her next movie for the last month, applying herself diligently, making notes, doing research, talking to the writer and director. There was nothing casual about Ardith's approach to her work. She examined it emotionally and intellectually and brought all her years of experience to each role. Josh had much to learn from her and she was an excellent teacher. She said it was one of the few advantages of age.

Ardith and Josh went to three of the most important after-parties. Everywhere they went, the crowds went crazy over Ardith. It was scary sometimes, and Josh was afraid she'd get hurt, but she handled each fan and each situation with grace. She was a consummate professional, and he was in awe of her, observing her public persona, which he had never seen at close range before. She lived in an isolated bubble, and he was part of that now, and tonight was his debut in her much bigger public world. He was beaming with pride wherever they went. And he was just modest enough to step backward and let her shine, which endeared him to the press. He could have played the role of the hot young guy, strutting his stuff, but he didn't. He was natural and friendly and warm, and didn't let the adulation of the press turn his head. He had won his place at her side honestly, by being himself, which was what Ardith loved about him, and so did the media.

She told the reporters about the movie he was working on, and told them to keep an eye on him, he would be a big star one day. And they believed her. He had the looks and the charm and the talent, and now he had her. He had everything he needed to be a huge success, and he had the most famous agent in Hollywood, thanks to her. She had opened all the right doors for him, and he had walked through them on his own merit, which made him worthy of respect.

They were both tired when they got home that night and found Oscar snoring happily on their bed. They didn't have to jump out of bed in the morning before Benicia arrived anymore. She had figured it out, and by now politely ignored the situation without comment. And Josh was always nice to her.

"Wow, that was incredible," Josh said with a grin, as he undid his bow tie and took off his shoes. Ardith had given him a set of cufflinks and studs before they went out that night. They were simple black enamel with a tiny diamond in the center and had belonged to Cary Grant. She'd bought them for Josh at auction at Sotheby's. She thought Josh looked a little like Cary Grant, in a bigger, younger, more modern version. He had his own sense of style and had looked very elegant that night. She had thought of everything to put him forward and make him feel comfortable, and he was living up to her faith in him. He felt like a man at her side, worthy of respect, not a cabana boy or a young boyfriend. He had money in the bank from the movie he was making, and had given up his apartment and moved in with Ardith. Joe Ricci had told her that Josh had worked for her for free when the producer stopped paying him, and she was deeply touched.

At forty-one, he was a respectable age, not twenty-five. They looked handsome together, and not ridiculous, which was a relief to her. He was growing into his new role with ease and grace. "I don't think there's anything you can do to top this evening," Josh said, still in awe of everything he'd seen that night and been part of, as she took off the gold dress. She had looked spectacular at his side, and every inch the legendary star she was. He still couldn't believe that he was there with her. Someone had compared them to Hollywood's updated version of Grace Kelly, with her sleek blond looks, and Cary Grant in his youth. It wasn't a hard comparison to live with. "Thank you for making everything so easy for me," he said gratefully as he kissed her. He didn't take any of it for granted, which touched her. Other men in her life had either resented her stardom and punished her for it, or been jealous of her. Josh wasn't. He was just thrilled to be there with her, and it showed. "What are we doing tomorrow?" he asked her, as she took off her makeup and he brushed his teeth.

"Going to the gym, you have your drama coach, I'm taking Oscar to the groomer, and Benicia and I are cleaning out the laundry room. We need new sheets."

"You lead a glamorous life," he said, as he kissed her and followed her to bed. "I think people imagine that you lie around the house in satin peignoirs with marabou feathers, drinking martinis and watching old movies."

"How depressing." She made a face. "If I ever get to that, shoot me." She looked pensive then, as they got into bed. They were both exhausted, it had been a long night for both of them. She couldn't let her guard down for a minute. She had been on public display, under intense scrutiny for nine hours, and so had he. "I want to go to New York one of these days and see Morgan, now that things have settled down. I want to meet Ben, if she's serious about him. I don't know if it will last, but it sounds like she is."

"Did that monster disappear?"

"I think so. Getting arrested for fraud and extortion must have cooled her off. Morgan thinks she'll have an abortion since her scheme didn't work. She must be an ingenious, conniving little bitch."

"There are plenty of those out there," Josh commented, "though not as extreme as she is. And he's a big target."

"Remember that," Ardith said seriously. "You're going to be a target now too. Don't be alone with some starlet in a compromising situation. There will be women who want to take advantage of you and can accuse you of anything that serves the purpose."

"It's a scary thought," and it had occurred to him too. "I don't see myself that way, as a useful opportunity."

"Maybe not, but others will." It was sad that they both had to be so careful, but Ardith had no illusions about it after forty years in the business, even at a gentler time in the beginning. There were bad people out there, willing to do anything to get ahead at someone else's expense. It happened to her in big and small ways all the time, lies in the press, padded bills, malevolent, dishonest people who would prey on any vulnerability that served their purpose, just as Tracy McCarthy had done to Ben, even though she was an extreme case. Ardith thought Tracy had to be a little crazy to do what she had. She had been willing to go to inordinate lengths to use Ben and make a lot of money. And she was only twenty-two.

Josh cuddled up next to Ardith, and they talked about the evening, as Oscar continued to snore next to them, and moved from her pillow to his. They were best friends now. Even Benicia had adjusted to the new regime, after a few tears and disapproving looks at first, when she realized that Josh had moved into Ardith's bedroom and her life. Benicia hadn't forgotten Bill, and neither had Ardith. There was a handsome photograph of him with Ardith in the living room, and another one at the peak of his career long before she met him. He had never been one of Hollywood's biggest stars or greatest talents, but he had had a long solid career, and the respect of his peers.

Her life was entirely different with Josh now, younger and more active, more like what it had been in her thirties and forties, and she loved it.

The morning after the Academy Awards, they went for a run together. Josh was dogged about keeping her healthy, eating right and exercising more than she had in years, and her body looked terrific for her age. She looked like she had dropped twenty years since she'd been with him.

"It's all the sex," she said mischievously over breakfast after their run. He had made her an evil-looking green drink, he blended one for her himself every morning. She had no idea what was in it, and said she didn't want to know, but she drank it to please him. It was full of leafy green vegetables and lime juice. He had almost completely eliminated sugar from her diet. And he left for the gym shortly after breakfast. His shoulders were broader and stronger than ever from his workouts, which would look great on-screen. He had the day off shooting and wanted to spend time with Ardith. He planned to drive out to the beach with her on his Harley, after she and Benicia finished their inventory of the sheets. He kissed her on the fly as he left, and Morgan called her a few minutes later.

"You looked fabulous in that gold dress, Mom," Morgan complimented her.

"I borrowed it, like Cinderella," her mother chuckled. "It's going back today. I'd buy it, but it costs a fortune." Ardith wasn't frugal, but she was sensible about what she purchased, and she couldn't have worn it publicly again, it was too memorable, and a star of her magnitude couldn't be seen in the same gown twice. She had worn quieter clothes when she went out with Bill. They were a dignified older couple. She had gone all out the night before. And most of the stars at major Hollywood events wore borrowed gowns and jewels that were worth a fortune that they couldn't afford and that made a big impact.

"You took Josh with you?" Morgan said cautiously. She had been wondering about him lately. He seemed to be around a lot, and she knew he had gone back to acting and was working on a movie, which her mother said was a good one. So, he was no longer her assistant, but he still seemed to be present on a regular basis, and she assumed they were friends. But when she saw him at the Academy Awards, they looked like a couple, and Ardith looked youthful and discreetly intimate on his arm.

"I did take him," Ardith said calmly, wondering if now was the time to tell her daughter that things had changed. Josh had been there for more than two months, and Bill had been gone for almost as long. "It was a big deal for him," Ardith said casually, easing into the waters, and not sure how Morgan would react. She had objected to Josh before, but Ben was in Morgan's life now, and they had been through a shocking experience together, which might have mellowed Morgan, although Ardith knew how harsh Morgan could be in her judgments, particularly on the subject of her mother. But Morgan had seemed gentler lately, with her own problems, and Ben's, to think of. And there was a huge discrepancy between her age and Ben's, which Ardith hoped might have softened her view on the subject.

"He looked very handsome," Morgan said about Josh.

"He spends his life in the gym now that he's working on a film again. He's playing the supporting lead, and Joe is representing him."

"That was nice of you."

"Everybody deserves a chance, and this isn't an easy business. Lucky for him, he looks young for his age, and can still play thirty-year-old parts. And they're not as tough on men as they are on women in this business. I'm lucky Joe got me a part in my new movie. It took a hell of a long time to find the right one this time."

"You'll always find great parts, Mom," Morgan said generously. She was on her lunch break and had time to chat as she ate a yogurt at her desk. She was curious about something and working up to it. "Can I ask you a question?" She finally dared to broach the subject, though it was delicate and she didn't want to get in an argument with her mother. They had been getting along ever since she'd told her about Ben, and his troubles, and their relationship. Things had shifted since her trip to Paris, and Morgan wondered if Amanda had given her useful insights into her mother with what she said about her own. "This probably sounds crazy," Morgan said, not sure how to ask her without starting a riot, or prying, "but is something going on with you and Josh?" There was a long silence while Ardith debated whether or not to tell her the truth. But it was becoming obvious, and she and Josh had been fairly open at the Academy Awards the night before. And he was living with her now. She had to tell Morgan sooner or later, and now might be the time, before the press grabbed it and ran with it, which seemed imminent. They had very clearly been a couple at the awards, and the press ate it up. They liked them both, and Josh had handled it well.

"Yes," Ardith said quietly, waiting for the storm to hit. "Things just kind of happened naturally and evolved. He's an old soul, and a good man," she justified it, but lightning didn't strike, which amazed her, and she heard Morgan sigh.

"I thought so, but was afraid to ask. I've been so upset and worried about Ben, I think I missed all the signs, and it sounds stupid, but I was angry at you all the time. I think I've acted like an angry adolescent with you for a long time. But you're you and I'm me, and I think we've missed some opportunities because I was mad at you that you weren't around more when I was a kid."

"I know you were, and you were right. I've always regretted it, but I couldn't get close enough to you later to make it up to you. What changed?" Ardith was stunned. It was the most adult conversation they'd ever had.

"I don't know. It's too energy-consuming to be pissed all the time, and being with Ben has taught me a lot. I don't know if we'll stay together, but nothing's perfect, and I think we both grew up, from dealing with what happened to him when that monster tried to blackmail him."

"Have you forgiven him?" Ardith asked her. "And figured out the timing?"

"I believe that he was telling the truth. It happened right before we met. It was a stupid thing to do, but he almost paid a terrible price and could have lost his career over it. I don't think he'd do it now, and he loves me. I love him too."

"Do you care about his age?" Ardith asked her.

"Honestly? No. I like it, even if he made a stupid mistake, and he drives me crazy sometimes when he gets busy and disappears. I love him, and I like that he's an adult with a major job, and I understand the pressures on him because of what I've seen you go through over the years. He's a star in his own world. And I have my work to ground me. I don't have to get caught up in his stardom. I can still be me, and he respects that. Younger guys are always jealous of my work, or think I work too hard, or want to compete with me. Ben doesn't, he has his own career to worry about, and he respects mine. Even if he's been sloppy as hell about his love life before this, I've never felt as respected by a man. He doesn't see me as a threat. That's hard to find these days, for any woman with a successful career. What about you and Josh? Do you think he's in it for what he can get out of it?"

"No, I don't," Ardith said. "He's his own man, and he's not threatened by me either. Every other man in my life has been, except Bill. Even your father was, and he was as big a star as a director and producer as I was then as an actress, but he was jealous of my success, which is why he was always dabbling with starlets, because they were impressed by him, and he thought I wasn't. Male egos are very fragile in my business. Josh is solid. Bill respected me too, but he was old and winding down, and he was never as ambitious as I am. I still want to pursue my career. I can be myself with Josh, and he makes me feel young, weirdly. You'd think being with someone younger would make me feel old, but it doesn't. We have fun together, and we feel like equals on a personal level. I've never had that before." She was being honest with her daughter for the first time, about who she was, and she liked the way it felt. And so did Morgan.

"I think that before Ben, I would have been shocked about you and Josh," Morgan said. And maybe before meeting Amanda, who had such a healthy, tolerant view of her parents. She was leading her life the way she wanted to and respected their right to do the same. "But I'm not shocked now. I'm happy for you if he's good to you. And I know that one day, Ben will be old before I am, but for now I don't care, and maybe I won't care then. I don't want to give him up because of what might happen twenty years from now. Maybe he'll be terrific until a great age. People live longer, in better shape now, and I hope he does. Who knows, I might fall apart before he does."

"I was worried about it with Josh at first," Ardith said, "but he really doesn't seem to care. It's hard being older, as a woman, and I don't want to look ridiculous or pathetic, to him or the world. But when we're together it doesn't seem to matter, and the playing field is pretty even. I can teach him about the business we're in, and he teaches me a lot about life. He isn't jealous of me, which makes a big difference. He accepts me as I am. It sounds crazy. I should be with someone Ben's age, and you should be with Josh. It really is upside down, but the funny thing is it works. And you don't pick who you fall in love with. One day it hits you, with the last person you thought you would love, and suddenly it all makes sense. I've been meaning to tell you about us, but to tell you the truth, I didn't have the guts, and I wanted to enjoy it without fighting with you."

"Me too," Morgan said and laughed, as she finished her yogurt. "Maybe age just doesn't matter anymore, or maybe we both got lucky and found the right people."

"I hope he is right for you," Ardith said gently about Ben.

"This whole blackmail mess threw me for a while," Morgan confessed to her mother, "but we're getting back to normal now."

"It taught you both how you function together in a crisis," Ardith said wisely. "That's important too. You didn't stomp off and ditch him. You stuck by him, and I'm sure he appreciates it, at least I hope so."

"He does," Morgan said. "We'll come out for a weekend sometime so you can get to know him, maybe before you start your picture. I know you'll be busy after that." She didn't resent it now, it was part of her mother's job, just like her heavy work schedule was part of her own adult life. She had Ben now. She didn't need to be angry at her mother for the past, or react to her like a teenager anymore. "I'd better get back to work," Morgan said. "I've got back-to-back Botox shots all afternoon. I send a lot of them to dermatologists, but my regular patients like to come to me for their shots. I'm happy we talked, Mom, and good for you with Josh. We can go bowling together," Morgan teased her, and they both laughed. "I'm sorry I made a fuss about that."

"He has me on health foods, it's disgusting."

"Good for him. I want you to live forever, Mom. I think being happy keeps people young, better than surgery. I love you. Talk to you soon."

Ardith was still smiling after the call and was in a good mood when Josh came home from the gym.

"You look happy," he commented when he kissed her. He'd had a good workout, which always relaxed him.

"I am. I talked to Morgan."

"Now that's a contradiction," he said, intrigued.

"She asked about you, and I told her."

He looked stunned and wary. "Did she go nuts?"

"No. I think it's the first adult conversation we've ever had. She wasn't pissed, I don't even think she was surprised. She saw us at the awards last night, and it was pretty obvious that we're together. I think she's grown up a lot with this mess with Ben. She said she's happy for us, and they'll come out for a weekend sometime, so we can meet Ben, and they can get to know you better."

"Everything he went through must have been brutal for them." Josh smiled, looking at the woman he loved. He was happy for her that Morgan had accepted them and hadn't been hard on her mother.

"We agreed that life is crazy. She should be with you, and I should be with him. But this is who we fell in love with and it works for us, no matter what anyone thinks."

"And I'm not trading places, just so you're clear on that. I admire your daughter, and her work, but she's a handful."

"You've seen her at her worst, around me," Ardith said quietly.

"I just want her to be good to you. I don't know what happened when she was young, but you're a wonderful mother to her now, patient and loving and forgiving. You deserve her love and respect."

Ardith laughed. "That's what she said about you."

She finished her laundry room inventory while Josh worked with his drama coach that afternoon, and then they went to the beach on his Harley. He had bought her a pink Barbie doll helmet and goggles of her own. They took a long walk on the sand, holding hands, and talking about the small miracles in life, like finding love and the right person, at whatever age you found them. It really was a miracle at any age. And Ardith was happy that Morgan had grown up and forgiven her at last. It was time.

Chapter 15

Morgan and Ben were gently easing back into the relationship they'd started before the bomb of Tracy McCarthy had hit their life. She was out on bail, pending the fraud and extortion charges, and Ben hadn't heard from her again. She was being represented by the public defender and the trial was still a long way off, unless she changed her plea to guilty, but there had been no word of that.

Ben was busy pursuing his career and had had a good talk with the head of the network. He understood what had happened, and was relieved that Ben had learned a hard lesson and wouldn't be as indiscriminate about his liaisons in the future. Ben had told him about Morgan, and the network head was pleased for Ben. He said Ben needed stability in his life, and a good steady woman, and Morgan sounded like she was, from Ben's description of her.

Their relationship was solid, and Tracy was out of their lives now, and possibly working on some other get-rich-quick scam at someone else's expense, but not Ben's.

Morgan's own schedule was very heavy at the moment, and Ben's French presidential special had gotten high ratings. They wanted to go to L.A. for a weekend but hadn't had time. Ardith was preparing for her new film, and Josh was shooting his movie. All four of them had busy lives.

Morgan had an emergency surgery one afternoon on a ten-year-old boy who had gotten a bad gash on his chin while playing soccer, and as his mother was one of her patients, she had agreed to operate on him so the gash didn't leave a bad scar. She was just coming out of the surgery when she saw several nurses and doctors raptly watching the TV in the surgical staff lounge.

"What happened?" she asked as she walked by and pulled off her surgical cap. Regular programming had been interrupted for a news bulletin. Someone had been shot, but she didn't know who at first. All she could see was a cluster of police cars outside an office building and an ambulance shrieking away with sirens blaring and flashing blue lights. And then she recognized the building and stared at the screen with the others.

"Ben Ryan was shot," one of the nurses filled her in, and Morgan felt as though there was a vise gripping her heart.

"Is he alive?" Morgan asked in a choked whisper.

"I think so, just barely. Some lunatic got into the building. She was a temp there and knew where his office was and how to get in through an employee door. She used an expired employee badge to get in, went to his office, and shot him in the chest. The paramedics came right away." The nurse reiterated what they'd heard.

"Where did they take him?" Morgan asked urgently. No one on staff knew that she was Ben's girlfriend. They had no reason to, since Morgan was discreet about it.

"NYU, I think." Morgan ran out of the room and headed for the stairs to the lobby. She didn't want to wait for the elevator. She knew her way out of the building down back stairs and back passages and grabbed a cab waiting in line outside of the building and told him to take her to NYU Medical Center. She had an ID badge around her neck, and a little money in her pocket, but she hadn't stopped to get her purse out of her locker. She didn't even have her phone on her, so she couldn't call to confirm that he was at NYU but asked the driver if she could use his.

"I'm a doctor. It's an emergency," she said with a pleading look, and he handed it to her with a glance in the rearview mirror. He had thought she was a nurse in her scrubs. She called the doctors' line at NYU and confirmed that Ben Ryan had been admitted to the trauma unit.

Morgan handed the phone back, paid the driver with a huge tip, and leapt out of the cab when they got to the emergency entrance of NYU Medical Center.

"Good luck!" the driver called after her, and she ran inside, asked for the trauma unit, and was breathless when she got there.

"I'm a doctor," she explained at the nurses' desk when she asked for Ben. "His personal physician." She thought it would give her easier access than saying she was his girlfriend.

"He's in surgery," the head nurse said.

"Can I see the chart?" Morgan asked, trying to sound professional and calmer than she felt.

"It's with him. Chest wound, gunshot wound, at close range," the nurse said grimly. "You'll have to wait till after the surgery to speak to the surgeon," she said. News crews were already gathering out-side and filling the lobby, and there were police filing into the trauma unit. Morgan asked one of them what had happened, and because she was in surgical scrubs, he told her more than he would have oth-erwise.

"The suspect apparently knew him. Twenty-two-year-old female. She'd been an intern at the network. She's in custody. We don't know the details or the motive yet. She'll be charged with attempted mur-der. She aimed straight for his heart, with a small handgun. She got past the metal detectors, don't ask me how, by some back door she knew, with an old badge." If what he said was true, Morgan knew that Ben's chances of survival were slim, shot in the chest at close range. There was nothing she could do medically. All she could do was sit in the waiting room and pray for him.

It was six o'clock by then, and ten o'clock when one of the nurses came to tell her that the surgeon had just gotten onto the floor and could talk to her. She went to the desk to see him, and identified herself as a physician, which he could see from her own hospital badge.

"He's in recovery now. He did well. He's a lucky guy, and fortu-nately the shooter was no expert with a handgun. She aimed at his heart from across his desk, at an angle—the bullet grazed his chest, exited, and lodged in his arm. She nicked an artery and he lost a lot of blood before we got to him. He could have bled out, but he didn't. The paramedics saved him. There was no heart or lung damage, and no permanent damage to the arm. He's had four transfusions, and he's going to be okay. Apparently he knew the girl, some kind of stalker or something. She had it in for him. She definitely tried to kill him. The police know the details, and the shooter is in custody. She'll be up for attempted murder on this one," he said, shaking his head.

"Can I see him?" Morgan asked, looking anxious, and the surgeon hesitated, and then nodded.

"Since you're a doc, I can make an exception. He's still pretty groggy. We're keeping him in recovery tonight, and we'll move him to Trauma ICU tomorrow. We want to keep an eye on him, to make sure the artery doesn't spring a leak, but he's in good shape, and seems healthy for his age. He should be fine."

"Thank you," Morgan said, feeling breathless, and her knees were shaking. Ben could easily have bled to death when the bullet hit his artery. He was lucky to be alive.

The surgeon took her to the surgical floor himself and let her into the recovery room, where a resident and three nurses were taking Ben's vitals and keeping him under close supervision. Ben was talking to them intermittently and dozing off, and Morgan could see that he was still heavily drugged. The surgeon explained to the team assigned to Ben that she was his personal physician, and then winked at them, and they smiled. She was obviously more than just Ben's doctor, as she leaned her face close to his and kissed him.

"Hi . . . how do you feel?" she asked in a whisper, as the team stood around him. Ben looked surprised to see her.

"I feel good . . . how do you feel?" he asked her, and they smiled.

"I'm glad you're okay. I love you."

"I love you too," he said. "I can't feel my arm, it's really heavy."

"They fixed you up, it'll be fine." She knew it was still numb from the surgery.

"I think I was shot." He remembered that much but looked confused. The lines in his face seemed deeper and he was very pale. They were still administering the fourth transfusion.

"We can talk about it tomorrow. Try to sleep. Okay?"

"Okay. And I don't want a face-lift. Okay?" He turned to the nurse closest to him. "She's a plastic surgeon, a very good one." They all smiled at that.

"No face-lift, I promise. Just sleep. I love you," she told him again, and withdrew. He needed rest and the nurses needed to do their job. The surgeon was still standing by and she thanked him when she left, and then she thought of something. She went to one of the doctors' phones in the hallway and asked to be connected to Labor and Delivery. Perry Blackstone practiced at NYU and might be there for a delivery. He came on the line immediately.

"What are you doing here?" he asked her. He sounded happy to hear her.

"Ben was shot. I'm in surgical trauma. I don't know for sure, but it sounds like Tracy did it."

"Jesus, that woman is insane. Is he okay?"

"He will be. She shot him in the chest, and the bullet hit an artery on exit. He's pretty out of it, he's in recovery. They just finished."

"Do you want to come down for a cup of coffee? I'm in L and D, with twins, but she's just had an epidural, and I've got a few minutes."

"Maybe tomorrow, it's been a long night."

"I heard that some reporter was shot, I didn't realize it was Ben. The cops are all over the building. Poor guy, he definitely got more than he bargained for with her."

"She's going to be charged with attempted murder," Morgan informed him.

"Nice way to bring a baby into the world, if she hasn't gotten rid of it yet." Perry was sure she would when her plot to extort money from Ben didn't work. For someone like her, the baby was disposable, and only a means to an end. "I'm sorry, Morgan. I know you care about Ben. He's a good guy."

"Yes, he is. He didn't deserve all this." All she wanted now was for him to survive and recover.

"Call me if you come back to see him. If I'm here, we'll have coffee." She could hear more than friendly interest in his voice. She had always liked him, and might even have gone out with him, but the timing had always been wrong for one or the other of them, and it still was. She realized now how deeply in love she was with Ben, and however crazy the last few months had been, she thought he was worth it. And she trusted him again.

She took a cab back to NewYork-Presbyterian Hospital a few minutes later, and had the driver wait for her while she went to get her purse and retrieve her phone, and then take her to her apartment. She saw when she checked her phone that her mother had called her seven times, and it was still early enough to call her in California. It was only eight o'clock for Ardith, and eleven in New York.

"Hi, Mom," Morgan said when Ardith answered.

"Oh my God. We saw on the news what happened to Ben. Is he okay?"

"Yes, I just saw him after his surgery. He lost a lot of blood, but there's no heart or lung damage, thank God. She shot him in the chest, and the bullet hit an artery on the way out. They got him to the hospital in time."

"Is it that same awful girl who tried to blackmail him?"

"I think so. I don't know any of the details. I ran to the hospital where they'd taken him as soon as I saw it on TV. I'd just come out of surgery myself."

"Poor man. I was so afraid he wouldn't make it when I saw it on TV. I called you but you didn't pick up."

"I didn't have my purse or my phone with me. I took off in my scrubs with a little money in my pocket to the hospital where they'd taken him. I'm on my way home now. I just picked up my phone."

"Let us know how he is," Ardith said, deeply concerned for both of them, "and watch out for that girl!"

"She's in custody. She's not going anywhere now."

"Except straight to prison, I hope," Ardith added, and they hung up.

"How is he?" Josh asked her, deeply concerned. They'd been worried about him all night, even though they didn't know him.

"Morgan says he'll be okay. He lost a lot of blood, but no major damage. She certainly won't be bored with Ben in her life," Ardith said, relieved that Ben had survived. "Apparently, he was in a bombing in India several months ago and was injured. He leads a dangerous life, but she loves him."

Josh put an arm around Ardith and hugged her. She had been worried sick about Morgan, particularly when she couldn't reach her. She was afraid Ben might have died.

"Let's go to New York soon," Ardith said to Josh over dinner.

"When he recovers, and you have a break. I want to meet him, before something else happens to him," she said, and Josh smiled. They had both been shocked when they heard about the shooting on the news.

Ben was fully awake when Morgan went to see him the next day before she went to work. He still looked pale, but better than he had the night before. She peeked into his room and he smiled broadly as soon as he saw her.

"Hi there." He smiled and kissed her when she got to his bed. "Did I see you last night?" He wasn't sure. He thought he'd been dreaming.

"You were pretty groggy from the surgery. You told me you didn't want a face-lift. You don't need one."

"No, just a bodyguard, with that lunatic on the loose. She's in custody now, though. She was pissed that she got no money from her baby scam and that I filed charges against her. She showed up in my office, found me alone, told me I deserved to die, and shot me."

"She'll be gone for a long time for this," Morgan said, relieved.

"I was sure she'd kill me when she pointed the gun at me," he said quietly. "All I could think of was you, and then I heard the gun go off, and I don't remember anything after that. She aimed it right at my heart."

"Thank God she missed," Morgan said, holding his hand. "Do you need anything? Are they giving you enough pain meds?" she asked.

"I just want to go home. I feel okay."

"Don't rush it, they want to be sure the artery is solid, that's a delicate repair. I'm sure they'll let you come home in a few days," she said, and he smiled at her.

"You're the best thing that ever happened to me, Morgan."

"So are you, but we need a little smooth sailing for a while." He nodded. It was what he wanted too.

"I called Amanda this morning in case she heard it on the news. She hadn't, and she asked about you. She likes you a lot."

"I like her too." Even though their lives were very different, Morgan could imagine their being friends. Amanda was a bright, sensible woman, and she loved her father, quirks and all.

"She wasn't too happy that I'd been shot," he said, and Morgan laughed.

"I don't suppose she was. Neither was I. I almost died when I saw it on the news. I came down here at a dead run. You were already in surgery. I saw you in recovery after that."

"I saw Perry Blackstone early this morning. He came to say hi after he delivered twins. I think he has a crush on you," Ben said with a worried glance at Morgan.

"We were good friends in med school, but it was never a romance," she reassured him.

"I think he'd like to change that," Ben said quietly.

"It's too late. I'm in love with you, with your crazy life, and women hitting on you and shooting you, and blackmailing you, and getting in hotel explosions in Delhi. Do you think we have a shot at any kind of peaceful life?" she teased him, and he grinned.

"Probably not. It's been a little crazier than usual lately."

"Maybe I should keep a medical kit at the apartment. I love you, Ben Ryan, no matter how crazy your life is."

"Even though I'm an old man? You should be with someone like Perry. I thought that when I saw him this morning, and you're both physicians."

"I'm not in love with him. I'm in love with you. And you're not an old man."

"I feel like one today."

"Well, you're not. Old men don't get shot by twenty-two-year-old interns or run around the world interviewing presidents. And I'm not in love with an old man. I'm in love with *you*," she said simply, and meant it. "Just try to keep it down to a dull roar, so you don't make an old woman of me. I aged about ten years last night. I need you, Ben. I love you. Try to stay in one piece," she said, and he leaned over and kissed her and winced.

She got his breakfast tray for him, and the surgeon came to check on him and was pleased at his progress. And Ben's vitals were stable.

"I think we can send you home in a few days. I hear you have excellent medical care at home," the surgeon said, smiling at Morgan.

"The best," Ben confirmed. "And I have a trip to Iran scheduled in two weeks, into the mountains, to meet with the head of guerrilla forces there," Ben said, as though it was an average trip, which it was to him.

"I think you might want to postpone that for a while, a few weeks at least," the surgeon said with a glance at Morgan, and she nodded, and Ben laughed.

"I walked out of a bombed-out hotel in India last year," Ben said matter-of-factly.

"You must not get bored at home," the surgeon said to Morgan, and all three of them laughed. "Let's give this three or four weeks to heal and get you solid on your feet again, and then you can do whatever you want."

"We'll see," Ben said, not willing to make any promises, and Morgan gave him a warning look.

"I'm in charge until the doctor releases you," she said firmly, and Ben grinned at her wickedly.

"Is that so?"

"Yes, it is," she said, and he kissed her as soon as the doctor left. "Can you behave long enough for me to go to work?" she asked him, and he thought about it and nodded with a mischievous look.

"How soon will you be back?"

"At lunchtime. I'm going to have them sedate you if you don't stay in bed and take it easy."

"I want to go home with you," he said longingly.

"Soon."

"I need to call my office and find out what's going on."

"Tell them you're not going to Iran." She left the room as soon as he called them, and she could see the life she had in store with him, of constant excitement, big stories all over the world, the pressures of his job, meetings with heads of state, travels to war zones. Ben Ryan wasn't going to stop running for a very long time, and life would never be peaceful. There was no risk of that. Even getting shot in the chest hadn't slowed him down. There was nothing old about Ben.

Chapter 16

J osh's movie wrapped two weeks before Ardith's next picture was about to begin. He wanted to take her to Venice for a few days, which sounded heavenly to her. They were going to stop in New York for two days on the way, to see Morgan and finally meet Ben.

He was back on his feet. Tracy McCarthy had pled guilty to a reduced charge of attempted second-degree murder and was awaiting sentencing in custody. They knew now that she had a history of mental instability and had spent a year in a psychiatric hospital at seventeen for violent behavior. The nightmare was truly over. Morgan had complained to her mother that she couldn't keep Ben down. He had canceled the trip to Iran and gone to Manila instead, and to Rabat to interview the new king of Morocco, who was making important political changes in the country, which set an example for others, and who had taken a harsh stance on terrorism.

Morgan could hardly keep up with him, but seemed happy, and

Ardith and Josh were eager to meet him. They stayed at the St. Regis, and had drinks at Ben's apartment and dinner at Majorelle. They were on their way to Rome for two days, and five days in Venice, as a romantic trip between their two films. Ardith was going to be in Zimbabwe on location in July, and Josh was going with her.

"So you don't fall in love with some young stud in the cast while you're on location," Josh told her. "I'm in my forties, you might replace me with a younger one," he said, and she assured him there was no risk of it.

The day before they left L.A., she had a gift delivered to him, to congratulate him for completing his first major movie. It was a vintage Harley with a sidecar. He loved it, and they drove around Bel Air in it, much to the annoyance of their neighbors, it was so loud.

The meeting with Ben and Morgan in New York went well. Ardith could see immediately why Morgan loved Ben. He was busy and vital and alive and important, and had his finger on the pulse of world events at all times. Ardith could tell that he was a risk-taker and lived on the edge, but she could also see that he adored her daughter. And Morgan had never been happier. Ardith could understand the attraction—he was exciting and handsome and brilliant, and despite their age difference, she had a feeling the relationship could work. He wasn't easy, but Morgan had her eyes open and knew that too, and was willing to take a chance on him. Ardith approved once she saw them together.

He and Josh hit it off, and Ben told them about some high spots to see in Zimbabwe if they got time off. Morgan thought it sounded awful, but Ardith was excited to go, and to have Josh with her on location. They had both learned from past mistakes what to avoid. Josh didn't want to be away from Ardith more than he had to, and she wanted to share all aspects of her life with him, not leave him behind. They trusted each other, but enjoyed each other's company too much to want to be parted for long. Josh was looking over scripts with her for his next movie, and valued her advice. He had read the script she'd been working on for months. She already knew all her lines, and the underlying nuances beneath them. They were both pros and loved their work. As did Morgan and Ben. Their careers were a major force in their lives, and as all four of them brought a lot to the table, they weren't expecting to feed off someone else. They were strong individuals, with deep respect for each other.

Ben was excited to meet Ardith, and impressed by her and Josh, and how well they got along. There was no dissonance between them, no envy, no competition. They were a couple based on love and mutual respect.

"They're really a team, and you can sense that they help each other and really love each other," Ben said after dinner, when Morgan went home with him. She was spending almost every night with him now, after nearly six months together, and he was feeling strong again. Almost too much so. He traveled almost constantly, interspersed by weeks at home with her. The travel was the nature of his job, when he interviewed world leaders, which was usual for him, but always exciting. He reminded her of a racehorse, dancing with excitement before he left, but also happy to cross the finish line and come home. And she loved her own work more than ever. It was satisfying and meaningful and rewarding, and she was going to do the project she wanted to in Vietnam in September, and Ben was going to try to find an excuse to join her. He knew the country well and wanted to visit it again with her. They had much to look forward to.

The two couples had lunch again the next day, and were old friends by the time Josh and Ardith left them that afternoon, to catch their flight to Rome and then Venice.

Josh chuckled on the way to the airport as he looked at Ardith.

"If we ever got married, would that make Ben my son-in-law?" He laughed at the idea and Ardith grinned at him.

"Not unless they get married too, and I don't think any of us want to get married," she said matter-of-factly.

"Why not?"

"Because none of us want kids. I'm certainly not going to have a baby, no matter what medical miracles they can pull off now. One child was enough for me, and I screwed that up pretty badly when she was young. And I think Morgan is phobic about marriage, and Ben isn't a fan of it either. He's already been married twice and doesn't seem to remember it fondly. Morgan could still have a baby, but doesn't want one."

"I'm still a virgin," Josh said virtuously. "I've never been married or had a baby."

"You're ahead of the game." And then she looked worried. "Are you wanting kids now?" It was one of her great fears that one day he would want children, and a woman who could give them to him.

"Only with you. Oscar is our only child," he said and kissed her. Benicia was taking care of Oscar while they were away and would do so again in July when they went to Africa. "It's too bad Morgan doesn't want kids. You'd be a cute grandmother. No, a very beautiful one," he corrected.

"You're crazy. Don't even think about it. I have absolutely no desire whatsoever to be a grandmother, or have a baby. Maybe we should get another dog for Oscar."

"He would hate it. He was born to be an only child," Josh said, as they got to the airport and checked their luggage. Ardith had been restrained and only brought two suitcases for the week, but she had an image to uphold, and they were staying at the elegant Cipriani in Venice. The trip was Josh's gift to Ardith and she was touched. He was very generous to her, now that he could afford to be. He had given her a red convertible vintage Mercedes sports car she drove everywhere, and he couldn't wait to drive around L.A. on his new Harley with the sidecar. They had fun together and expanded each other's lives. Morgan had noticed it too. They were playful, and Josh made her mother seem younger than she had in years.

By comparison, Morgan and Ben were more serious, but also had more serious jobs. But by nature both of them were sober, conservative people who dealt with complicated issues every day through their work. Both couples seemed well matched, and not as upside down as Ardith liked to claim.

Josh and Ardith took an overnight flight and arrived in Rome on a glorious golden morning, with the sun shining on the Vatican and the Basilica of Saint Peter.

They toured the usual tourist sites that afternoon, and stayed at the Hassler, where the staff knew Ardith well and gave her and Josh five-star treatment and a penthouse suite with a view of the city, just above the Spanish Steps and the Fontana della Barcaccia. They also went to the Fontana di Trevi, where Josh made Ardith toss a coin and make a wish and he did the same. He didn't tell her, but the wish was that they would live forever and be happy together. He could no longer imagine a life without her and had no reason to.

They found a beautiful little church while walking the city, and lit candles, and went shopping on the Via Condotti the next day. Ardith bought a very glamorous cocktail dress that Josh loved on her, and she bought him a black cashmere jacket at Armani that he could wear with jeans or when he was more dressed up, and that was suited to their life in L.A.

They were ready to leave for Venice two days later, and the honeymoon phase of their trip. Venice was pure magic, compared to the grandeur of Rome. It was small and mysterious. They walked for hours and took gondola rides. They drank wine and ate gelato in the Piazza San Marco. They took the speedboat back to the Cipriani across the lagoon when they were tired, and made love in the glamorous suite Josh had reserved for them. Everything about the trip was perfect, and they were sad to leave after five days, but Ardith had to get to work on her new movie, and it was arduous work.

She was up at four every morning, at the studio by five-thirty for hair and makeup, and on the set promptly at seven. She never missed a line, and worked closely with the director on each scene. Josh learned a lot just watching her and seeing how meticulous her performances were. He wondered if he would ever be half as good at acting as she was. She had combined raw natural talent that came from her soul with years of study and classes and experience to perfect her craft. She truly was the best actress in the business, as everyone said. She was a gift to watch, and Josh loved spending time on the set, observing quietly and admiring her work. They went home together at night and had dinner, and made love when she wasn't too tired. She poured every ounce of her being into her performances, and all of the cast said she was a joy to work with. And for all his teasing her about being a diva when they first met, she never was. She was the finest actress he had ever seen, and a remarkable human being. She was truly the love of his life, and he felt honored to be with her.

The cast and crew had a break in the schedule after seven weeks of shooting in L.A., before they left for Zimbabwe, and the production company had chartered a plane to get them there in luxurious comfort. They were going to be staying at one of the more famous safari camps, on an enormous game preserve, and they were planning to do a lot of night shooting, which was potentially dangerous. But they had plenty of guards and game wardens to protect them, local advisors, and members of the cast. There were half a dozen famous actors of Ardith's caliber, their entourages, and the vast number of people it took to shoot a major film. Josh was fascinated by the action, the people, and the location. He and Ardith had one of the best rooms in the main building, and he got to hang out with actors he had only seen on screen and never met. Ardith was very modest compared to many of them, and there were a number of British members of the cast and crew whom Josh enjoyed hanging out with, both older and younger than he was. He made no demands on anyone, and everyone liked him. And Ardith was proud to have him at her side. It made the time in Africa much more enjoyable for her. It allowed her to focus on her work, feel his constant support to make the job easier, and not worry about him feeling neglected at home, which would have stressed her, as it had when she left Morgan at home as a child, for which it had taken Morgan more than twenty years to forgive her mother. There was nothing to forgive this time, just the pleasure of being together and the immense satisfaction Ardith derived from her work. She was grateful to be there every day, learning from the others and the director, as he harnessed their respective talents and wove them together like fine gold thread.

Ardith and Josh were watching the sun come up one morning before she went to work. He got up with her every day, and they sat on the wide shaded veranda in enormous Nigerian white beaded chairs that she wished she could take home with her to L.A., but which seemed too cumbersome to ship and weren't for sale. There was so much she would have liked to take with her—the sunrises and sunsets in a blaze of brilliant color, the grace of the animals, the smiles of the children, the abundance of flowers, the warmth that the crew shared, which made everyone's work easier. It was a miraculous time that Ardith and Josh knew that they would never forget.

The cast and crew were going on location again in October, to finish shooting the film in England, and they were all looking forward to it. Ardith was considering another film that would start shooting in January, which would give her two months off between this picture and the next one. It seemed like enough time off, and Josh was looking at new scripts too. They had full months ahead to look forward to, and were determined to coordinate their schedules so they could be together. The one thing Ardith had learned long ago was that she didn't want to be separated from him. That was when problems happened, and she was determined to avoid that with him.

They were watching the sun rise on their last shooting day in Zimbabwe, and Josh turned to her with a solemn look.

"Let's get married," he said so softly that she thought she had misheard him or imagined it.

"What did you just say?" He repeated it clearly, with the sun coming up behind him. "Why?" was all she could think of to say, which wasn't the answer he wanted. He was serious, and meant it.

"Because we love each other. That's the only reason to do it, not for a baby or a house or a job. Just for us. As a confirmation that we believe in each other."

"I already believe in you," Ardith said simply.

"It means something. It's the final step in the love dance, like taking a bow." She smiled at what he said.

"I don't need to be married," she said to him.

"I think I do," he admitted. "For better or worse, and all that stuff. I'm discovering that I'm an old-fashioned guy."

"You really are, aren't you?" She smiled at him. There was something sweet about it, and she was touched. He got down on one knee then, in front of her, and asked her formally.

"Ardith Law, will you marry me?" She pulled him back to his feet. He towered over her and always made her feel small next to him.

"You might regret it one day," she said. "What if it ruins everything we have now?" They had only been together for eight months, and romantically for less than that.

"It won't ruin anything, it will strengthen it."

"How can you be so sure?" she said softly. She didn't want to spoil what they had. It was so precious to her.

"I just know it. I feel it in my soul. We belong together," he said with absolute conviction.

"We *are* together already."

"It's not the same," he said to her.

"Let's think about it."

"I already have. That's why I asked you."

"We'd have everyone's reaction to deal with, our friends, the public, the press, Morgan."

"Do you think Morgan would object?" He was surprised.

"I don't know. She certainly doesn't believe in marriage for herself, and neither does Ben. They're well suited that way."

"So are we," Josh said simply. "You believed in marriage the first time, and you got shortchanged. We wouldn't do that to each other. We're soulmates, no matter when we were born. I was born to be with you," he said with a certainty that moved her. "We could have been mother and son in another life, or father and daughter, sister and brother, best friends. But we were born to be husband and wife in this one. I'm sure of it."

"You just want me to promise to love, honor, and *obey* you." She tried to lighten the moment but he didn't laugh, he was serious, and she wanted to respect it. "I'll think about it. It's a big step, Josh."

"I know. That's why I asked you."

"I've only done it once in my life. I always thought that's how it should be."

"So do I. You won't have to do it again after this. When I'm old, and we die, I want to be married to you."

"You won't be old. I will be, and you'll live for years after I'm gone," she said seriously.

"You're going to live a long, long time," he said with almost mystical certainty. "Your spirit is young." She felt that way too, but it seemed odd to hear him say it.

Africa had been good for them, a powerful experience that had bonded them closer together. She went to work then, and they finished late that night, and went to bed, in the warm scented air of Africa. They could smell the flowers and the trees, the earth, and the animals. The scents were heady and dizzying at times.

They finished packing in the morning and were driven to Robert Gabriel Mugabe Airport in Harare to catch the plane home to L.A. Everyone was ready to go back, but they all admitted that they would miss the charm and beauty of Africa and hoped to come back one day.

"We could honeymoon here," Josh whispered to her, and she smiled. She could see that he meant it, and she liked the idea, if she agreed to marry him one day.

It was a long trip to L.A., and they changed planes in Johannesburg and Abu Dhabi in the United Arab Emirates, which already seemed very different from the game preserve where they'd lived for a month. They were going to shoot in L.A. for a month now, and then move the production to England in October.

It felt good to be home and see Oscar when they got there. He was miffed for a few days, but rapidly forgave them. Ardith had missed him, but she had been busy working. And the work on the film in September was intense. They shot a lot of hard scenes that required the actors' full attention and concentration on the emotions and the script.

She called Morgan on the rare days she was off and had time. The producers were pushing the cast hard so they could have the film edited and distributed by the end of the year to qualify for the Academy Awards and the Golden Globes.

Morgan said that she and Ben were fine. They'd been able to spend a week in the Hamptons in a house they rented. Ben's arm had healed well, and Tracy had been sent to prison for fifteen to twenty-five years.

Morgan left for her charitable project in Vietnam shortly after Ardith and Josh got back to L.A., so Ardith didn't hear from Morgan after that. Ben was meeting her there for the last week of her stay, and they were going to travel for a week together.

Josh didn't bring up marriage again after they got home, but Ardith knew it was on his mind. She could sense it.

He drove her around in the vintage Harley with the sidecar when she had a little time off, and picked her up on the set with it once. And everyone laughed when she put on her pink helmet and goggles and waved when they drove off. Josh added a light touch to her life as well as a depth she had never shared with anyone before. She knew that he was right, and they were soulmates. She felt it too, but she had no need to make it official. For her, it was enough just knowing it was true. She didn't need to prove it to anyone else.

Chapter 17

Josh and Ardith left for England right on schedule, to work on the final scenes of the movie. The whole production had been impeccably run, with military precision, and the producers were pleased. They hadn't gone over budget, which was unheard of.

The cast had a day off when they arrived in London and went to work the next day.

There was a small private airport near where they were shooting, which Josh went to explore, and he told Ardith the next day that he had met a pilot who was taking him up for free to fly over the whole area. There were several castles nearby and a famous abbey and Josh wanted to see it all from the air.

"Are you sure it's safe?" Ardith asked him when he told her that night.

"Of course. Small propeller planes are safer than jets. If something goes wrong, you just coast down and land in a field." She didn't like the idea, but she didn't want to mother him and stop him from doing something he enjoyed while she was working. There wasn't much to do in the area, and she was working long hours to finish the film. They were going to do postproduction in London, so Ardith would be free to go home when they were finished. But they had another month of hard work ahead of them.

Josh left for the small airport the next morning when she left for work. They were shooting in a famous castle, which had a gloomy feel to it, and the weather had turned chilly. She kissed him goodbye, and a car came to pick her up. He had rented a motorcycle to use while they were there. It was a beautiful old Ducati, which he was pleased with. He loved his vintage machines.

Shooting had gone slowly all day, and some of the actors were still tired from jetlag and forgot their lines. The director gave them a half-hour break to review the script, and they were all standing around the courtyard of the castle, chatting and smoking, when they heard a loud explosion in the distance, looked up instinctively, and saw a small plane explode into a ball of fire and plummet to the earth. Ardith screamed when she saw it, knowing that Josh was somewhere in the sky in the area in a small plane, and she suddenly knew to her very core that Josh had been on the one that burst into flame and crashed.

"Oh my God . . ." There were murmurs in the crowd, and the crew came outside to look. You could see black smoke coming from a field. Two of the crew members jumped into a truck they'd been using and took off in the direction of the field where the smoke was rising, to see if they could help.

Ardith wanted to go with them, but was afraid to, afraid of what she might see. She was sure that no one had survived the crash and that Josh was dead. One of the other actors said he thought he had seen a body fall out of the plane before it crashed, but he wasn't sure. Ardith was shaking and had to sit down. She had lost a husband to a helicopter crash, and now Josh. She didn't even know for sure that it was the plane he'd been on, but it seemed likely, and she didn't know the pilot's name or even what kind of plane it was exactly, just an old vintage plane Josh thought would be fun.

The two crew members came back with the truck half an hour later. They said the police were there, and an ambulance. The pilot had been killed, and they were keeping people away, afraid of another explosion from the fuel.

"Were there passengers?" Ardith asked weakly, and the crew members said they didn't know. The police had kept them from going any closer and didn't want to answer questions.

Ardith went to find the director and told him she wanted to leave, that Josh might have been on the plane that crashed and she had to find out. He told her to go right away, and one of the lighting crew drove her in a jeep they had on the set. Seeing the explosion and the crash had cast a pall on all of them.

They drove to the crash site first, and the police told her that there were no passengers they were aware of, but there could have been, and the explosion might have blown them out of the plane. But there were no other bodies found in the area. They drove to the small airport after that, and there were a dozen old planes lined up, all privately owned. There was a small office, and a few of the pilots were drinking coffee and talking about the crash. Ardith asked if any of them knew of an American who had chartered one of the planes for sightseeing that day. None of them had seen anyone of Josh's description, and they didn't know of any of the planes being hired for the day. They said there were three planes missing that afternoon, but the pilots who owned them were flying themselves. They tried calling them on their radios but no one answered. Their radios had a short range, and they must all have been out of range.

When Ardith got back to the manor house where they were staying, she didn't know if Josh was dead or alive. She went upstairs to lie down and wait to see if he came home. It was all she could do. Her head was throbbing and she felt sick to her stomach.

She got up when she heard the others come in, and went downstairs to meet them and tell them she had no news. But it was getting dark and Josh hadn't come back, which they all thought was a bad sign. They tried to encourage Ardith to believe that he would probably come home soon, but their eyes said something different.

Someone handed Ardith a glass of whiskey, and she sat down and took a sip, and closed her eyes. She was willing him to come back, and praying as she hadn't since she was a child. She couldn't lose him now.

She was holding the glass of whiskey with her eyes closed when she heard his voice. She didn't know if she had imagined it or if it was real, and she was afraid to open her eyes and see.

Josh saw her sitting there the moment he came through the door, and the others caught their breath as though they had seen a ghost. He strode across the room, knelt in front of her, and took her face in his hands. He had heard about the crash when he and his pilot landed, and he knew instantly what she must have thought.

She felt his hands on her face and opened her eyes and saw him in front of her, and dove into his arms as she broke into sobs. He took the glass of whiskey from her, set it down, and held her tightly.

"I'm okay . . . I'm here . . . I'm fine . . . I'm so sorry . . ."

"I thought you were dead," she sobbed, as the others discreetly left the room, grateful that he had returned. He held her until she stopped crying and looked at him with all the terror she had felt.

"I was wrong . . . I was so wrong . . . I do want to marry you . . . you were right." She had tried to hold back that one last bit, not to cast her whole heart into the basket and risk it again. But her heart and her life were already his. She had discovered it that afternoon. "I was afraid to marry you, but I'm not anymore."

"Good," he said, and they walked up to their room. It had been a terrifying afternoon, but it had led her the last step of the way.

She lay silently in his arms on the bed, and the tears continued to roll down her cheeks. Whatever the words or the ceremony or the traditions, they no longer mattered. There was no holding back. They already belonged to each other in all the ways that mattered, and she wanted to be his wife, for better or worse, until death do us part. And it nearly had, if it had been his plane that crashed and not another. They both realized how easily it could have been his.

Chapter 18

Ardith and Josh waited until she finished filming. They wanted to leave on a honeymoon afterward. They invited the whole cast and crew on the last day, in lieu of a wrap party. The ceremony was at the registrar's office in the village, and the reception was at the castle where they had been filming, with the same catering service that had been feeding them for a month. A local baker made the wedding cake. They were married by special license, which the embassy in London got for them since they qualified, having lived there for fifteen days prior to the registration and one full day after the ceremony was performed by the registrar, who was stunned by who the bride and groom were.

Ardith texted Morgan in Vietnam and told her what they were doing. It seemed simpler to do it here in the English countryside, far from paparazzi and all the press the wedding would draw if she and Josh got married in London or L.A. Morgan said she understood and wished them all the luck in the world.

The couple made their vows to each other, and Ardith wore a simple white wool dress she bought in a local shop. They bought plain gold bands at a local jeweler, and they both cried when the registrar pronounced them man and wife, and a cheer went up from the entire cast and crew surrounding them.

"It's a wrap!" Josh shouted in good Hollywood style, kissed her again, and carried her the length of the room and gently set her down outside the building, where they all hugged and kissed, and cried and laughed. And then the full group went back to the castle where they had worked hard and celebrated the end of the film and the beginning of Josh and Ardith's married life together. The toasts and speeches went on long into the night, and they drank the caterers dry of champagne and single malt whiskey. Most of the guests could hardly walk by the time they got back to their quarters at three o'clock that morning. It was a gentle night, and it had been the perfect wedding, full of joy and good spirits, and love for each other.

"Well, Mrs. Gray, we did it." Josh smiled broadly at her. Swaying slightly, he sat down in a big armchair in their room and pulled her onto his lap. "I never thought I'd be this lucky in my entire life," he said, and she kissed him. She'd had less to drink than he had but she was just as happy. "I promise you won't be sorry," he said solemnly.

"I know I won't." They were exactly what she had always dreamed of and never found: soulmates. They were meant to be together, regardless of the age difference between them. It truly didn't matter, nor did what anyone thought. The twenty-one years between them vanished when they were together. In this life or another, it wasn't upside down at all. It was precisely the way it was meant to be all along. He made her life fun and had given it purpose and meaning, and she had opened new horizons to him. It was what marriage should be, two people, loving partners and best friends forever.

About the Author

DANIELLE STEEL has been hailed as one of the world's best-selling authors, with a billion copies of her novels sold. Her many international bestsellers include *The Ball at Versailles, Second Act, Happiness, Palazzo, The Wedding Planner, Worthy Opponents, Without a Trace, The Whittiers,* and other highly acclaimed novels. She is also the author of *His Bright Light,* the story of her son Nick Traina's life and death; *A Gift of Hope,* a memoir of her work with the homeless; *Expect a Miracle,* a book of her favorite quotations for inspiration and comfort; *Pure Joy,* about the dogs she and her family have loved; and the children's books *Pretty Minnie in Paris* and *Pretty Minnie in Hollywood.*

daniellesteel.com
Facebook.com/DanielleSteelOfficial
Twitter: @daniellesteel
Instagram: @officialdaniellesteel

About the Type

This book was set in Charter, a typeface designed in 1987 by Matthew Carter (b. 1937) for Bitstream, Inc., a digital type-foundry that he cofounded in 1981. One of the most influential typographers of our time, Carter designed this versatile font to feature a compact width, squared serifs, and open letterforms. These features give the typeface a fresh, highly legible, and unencumbered appearance.